SHADES OF DARKNESS

NORA ASH

ONE

LIGHTNING

Rage. Blistering, all-encompassing rage mixed with fear so overpowering Lightning's knees nearly buckled as he stared at the note in his hand.

The glowing "B" carved into her desk was as good as leaving a business card, and it made Lightning's insides twist. Bright, the sociopathic supe who had risen out of nowhere two years ago to one of the top ranks in their hierarchy, had broken into Kathryn's home and fucking *kidnapped* her.

The anger was easy enough to deal with—he would just save it up until he found the scumbag, and then unleash it all in one, lethal round.

The fear... the fear was not so easy to manage.

He knew enough about Bright and the methods he'd used to climb the ladder for his stomach to knot at the thought of Kathryn—soft, *breakable* Kathryn—in his cruel hands.

A deep snarl tore him from the horrific scenarios the mere thought produced, and he spun around just in time to see a large, dark-clad figure crouch into a defensive position by the window.

"If you've hurt her, I'll rip your throat out!"

The Shade. The fucking *Shade*.

Lightning's hands flexed with desire to close around his enemy's neck, and the rage from realizing that his claimed human had been abducted took over, spiking his adrenaline with a primal urge to *kill*.

The note rustled with his hand's movement. Lightning paused, muscles tensed to strike. *The note.*

If he wanted Kathryn back, he needed The Shade.

A growl he couldn't control forced its way out of his chest as he straightened from his hunched pose. He wasn't entirely sure if it was disappointment of not being able to rip into his enemy, or if it was from the sickening knowledge that he needed The Shade's help to reclaim his human.

"Bright's got her."

The same shiver he'd felt himself when he spotted the carved "B" went through The Shade.

"*What?*" Anger clearly won out for the villain. His eyes blazed as he shifted, pulling the swords mounted on his back out of their scabbards. "*What?* What did you *do?*"

"Nothing, you imbecile. I just got here and found this." He pointed to the desk, where the carved letter shone faintly in the darkened loft.

The Shade glanced to the desk. He clenched his hands around the sword handles, making a barely detectable tremor travel down the blades.

"He left a note." Lightning dropped the piece of paper on the desk and stepped back to let his rival inspect it.

The Shade cast him a dark look before he stepped over and snatched it up.

His mouth spasmed once as his eyes flickered over the text. When he looked back up, the seething anger was mixed with concern—a rather startling expression on the infamous supe. "How did he know?"

Lightning rubbed a hand over his scalp, trying to ease the unpleasant prickle underneath the mask. All his hyped up senses were on full alert, making his suit feel restrictive.

"I don't know. Maybe he came to check her out because of that fucking article, maybe he has spies at the mayor's mansion and got curious when he saw her with me. Right now, it doesn't really matter. He's got her, and if we don't get her back..." He let the rest of the sentence hang suspended in the already tense air between them. There was no need to complete it—they both knew their society's rules. If a supe relinquished ownership of their human, it was the end of the road for her. It was the only way of ensuring their secrets were not exposed to the human world. If they didn't show up for the Council meeting, it would be the same as renouncing their claim.

"He has some balls." The Shade's growl was low and filled with the promise of murder. "After I'm done with you, I will rip them off before I kill him."

As much as Lightning's body ached to rise to the challenge, he clamped his jaw shut around his responding snarl in an attempt to stay in control of himself. "That's great. And after you're '*done with me*,' how are you going to convince the Council that she belongs to you? That's why he's got the balls to do this—technically, she doesn't belong to either of us without the other. The fucker knows we have to both show up and explain how we're sharing her, if we want her back."

And he also knew that it would be a cold day in hell before either of them admitted to being bound so tight by a mere human that they'd deign to work together, even for the duration of a Council meeting. Lightning glared at his enemy. *Fuck.* Not only would waltzing in there, hand in hand with The goddamn Shade, be the most humiliating thing he'd yet to endure—it would also broadcast with unwavering clarity that Kathryn was his one weak point. She'd never be safe again.

But if they didn't, she was as good as dead.

"Fuck!"

"She was all mine, until you marked her again." The Shade flexed his hands, probably to ease the same sort of agitation as was coursing through Lightning's veins at that moment. "He would never have gotten away with kidnapping a claimed human who only carried one mark."

Lightning narrowed his eyes into slits. "I claimed her first, if you recall. Don't remind me how you forced her to submit to you, or I'll forget I need you to get her back."

"If you had marked her properly, I could never have claimed her. You were too weak to take her, and you are too weak to give her what she needs. You want her back? She wasn't yours to begin with. You left her—twice!"

Guilt—that uncomfortable, new sensation in his gut—pulled on Lightning at The Shade's words. Yeah, he'd left her, because he was scared of her power over him, and now she was in danger. Again. The girl was a fucking magnet for trouble, and he should have stayed by her side, fear of the churning emotions she brought out in him be damned. Knowing she was in the hands of someone like Bright was much, much worse.

The guilt and shame tipped into anger, and he gratefully grabbed on with both hands. Anger, he knew how to deal with.

Lightning bared his teeth at The Shade. "She was mine when you took advantage of her fear and marked her, and she is mine now. And once she is safe, I will ensure that my mark on her neck is the only valid claim on her."

The Shade's nostrils pulled up with his responding snarl, but he nodded in acceptance of the challenge. "Once she is safe. But I'm warning you now—this time, I'm not holding back. You fight me for her, and you will die."

Despite his anger and the primal instincts pounding in his head, Lightning couldn't help but roll his eyes. They had fought more than once over the years, and there had never been a clear winner—which was the only reason they were both still alive. The hatred between them was too deep for mercy.

"Whatever you need to tell yourself. Until then, we need to focus on Bright. He isn't going to make it easy."

The Shade nodded again and crossed his arms over his chest. "He's undoubtedly hoping to humiliate us, possibly because he's heard I've been asking about him. And I suspect he'll attempt to convince the rest of the Council that because of the unique nature of her mark, our claims are invalid."

Lightning paused. The Shade was investigating Bright, too? "Why are you asking questions about him?"

The Shade leveled a condescending stare at him. "You think because I don't care who casts themselves up to be our leaders, I don't take notice when rumors start to circulate of a *new order*? Everything seems to come back to him. I imagine you're doing your own snooping."

Lightning nodded and pursed his lips. "The only way Kathryn's getting out of there alive is if we acknowledge that we share her."

The Shade's jaw twitched, but he didn't object. "I will

meet you at the Arena," he growled, stepping back toward the window without taking his eyes off Lightning. A dark flash, and he was gone.

It seemed it was, indeed, a cold day in hell.

Neither one of them paused to consider why they were willing to sacrifice their reputation over a human girl.

TWO

The room was cold. Cold and stark, with white walls, white linen on the single, metal framed bed, and a naked light bulb hanging from the ceiling. There were no windows to look through, and nothing to break up the white monotony.

Bright hadn't hurt me, apart from not being too gentle when he grabbed me from my home—and again when he shoved me into this room—but he hadn't told me what he had planned for me, either.

I thought the mark on my neck would keep me safe from other superhumans, but apparently, I'd been wrong. And so had both Lightning and The Shade.

So now, instead of being safely at home, watching TV and fretting about the two men who had claimed me, I was locked up God only knew where and kept prisoner by an unquestionably bad man.

I couldn't have been in there longer than a day at most, but already, my mind was starting to crack. I'd been scared ever since he revealed himself in my apartment, and the non-stop onslaught of adrenaline to my already frazzled nervous system was breaking down what little coping mechanisms I had for dangerous situations.

He'd said he would take me to a Council meeting to see if Lightning and The Shade would show up to claim me in front of everyone, but I didn't know when that meeting would be—nor did I know if either supe would even show up. Bright had made it sound like it would be shameful for them to admit to sharing me. I didn't know why, but regardless, I was pretty certain at least Lightning wouldn't go through any embarrassment to save me. He'd made it plenty clear that I wasn't all that important to him, after he'd bedded me.

That left The Shade.

A nervous flutter made me press my hand against my stomach. After what I'd discovered about his support of the mayor's secret weapons project, I wasn't so sure being saved by him would leave me much better off.

No, that wasn't true. I'd much rather be in the hands of a manipulative villain who seemed to care—if not about me, then about what was between my legs—than be killed because neither of my two lovers cared enough about me to endure some embarrassment.

Unfortunately, I couldn't do anything about my situation one way or the other—I literally just had to sit here, in the same panties and t-shirt I'd been wearing when I was kidnapped, and hope that either Lightning or The Shade were better men than they seemed.

THE DOOR CREAKING OPEN MADE me sit up on the bed with a start, heart pounding in my chest.

I'd been staring up at the ceiling, exhausted, hungry, and generally all-round miserable, for what felt like hours, until I'd finally dozed off.

Adrenaline cleared the fog of sleep as I pulled as far into the corner of my bed as I could get while staring at the door.

Bright stepped through, dragging a chair along with a mocking smile on his thin lips. "Don't worry, little mouse, I'm not going to ravage you. There's no need to look so scared —fat girls don't do it for me. But I can see that it's my esteemed colleagues' thing, so why don't we talk a bit about that, hmm?"

For once, being insulted about my weight didn't bother me in the least. I wouldn't go so far as to say I drew a breath of relief when he said he wasn't interested in me sexually. The possibility that I might get raped during my stay with Bright had definitely crossed my mind. After all, from what I knew of superhumans, they had a seriously hyped-up sex drive.

I eyed the villain carefully as he put the chair down and straddled it, leaning both arms on its back.

"So, Kathryn, what do you say you and I have a little chat?"

I remained silent, not wanting to show him how scared I truly was.

Bright narrowed his blue eyes in warning. "Do I need to remind you that it's in your best interest to stay on my good side? When I ask a question, I expect an answer, got it? I may not be allowed to harm you just yet, but once your two masters fail to claim you, your worthless body is all mine to dispose of. And if you don't cooperate, I'm going to make that very, very slow and painful. But if you do, maybe—just maybe—I'll let you live."

My lips quivered. I had no doubt he would make good on his threat, if Lightning or The Shade didn't save me... and I didn't have high hopes they would. But I didn't believe there was any chance he'd let me live—the best I could hope for was likely a swift death.

"What do you want to know?"

A self-satisfied smile curved his mouth, giving it a cruel slant. "That's much better. I knew you'd come around. What I want to know, Kathryn, is how you happened to end up with not one, but two claiming marks on that breakable little neck of yours?"

I bit my lip. As much as I wanted to give myself the best chances of survival, I didn't want to tell him anything that could help him with whatever diabolical plan he had going on with the mayor. And, I realized, much to my surprise, I didn't want to give away anything that might hurt Lightning or The Shade. Hopefully, telling him how they had claimed me wouldn't do either.

"Lightning claimed me first, to keep me safe after an article I wrote, but he didn't... didn't sleep with me. The Shade found me in an alley one night, and when I showed him the mark to warn him off, he decided to claim me fully himself. I think mainly to annoy Lightning."

Bright barked a surprised laugh. "Ha, I bet that worked well. Devious devil, that Shade. And I take it Lightning then decided to lay a full claim down, once he realized? The dual mark you've got doesn't suggest any half-claims."

I nodded, fighting down a blush from knowing that he was fully aware what both men had done to solidify their claims.

"Interesting. I don't think anyone ever realized you could layer marks like this, if the initial bite isn't accompanied by penetration. Undoubtedly because no one's ever been inter-ested enough in a human to even consider sharing." Bright leveled a curious look at me. "What is it about you that's got those two morons degrading themselves like this?"

My cheeks flooded with the heat I'd been trying to hold back, partly from humiliation and partly from anger. I'd had my own, private thoughts about not measuring up to the divine specimens who had shared my bed last night, but being told that they were *degrading* themselves by being with me was laying it on pretty thick. Okay, so I wasn't a vision of beauty, but it's not like I had begged them for their attention. Quite the contrary.

"I don't know," I gritted out between clenched teeth.

"Me either." Bright seemed completely unaware of, or disinterested in, my angry tone. "You're plain as plain can be, and yet two of the most powerful supes claimed ownership over you." He shrugged. "Or perhaps it's not about you, and they simply got caught up in their eternal rivalry. I suppose that is the likely explanation."

I didn't answer him, but I quietly agreed. What other reason was there, really? Certainly, they could both get all the women they pleased, whenever they wanted. Sure, Lightning's initial half-mark might have stemmed from pity, but everything that had followed? Rivalry was the likely answer to that mystery.

Said mark pulsed faintly as if in protest, but the dark wave of melancholy and self-pity that acceptance brought numbed even that.

I was nothing more than a passing fancy for either of them—a novelty to fuel their everlasting strife. It hurt more than it should have.

"Well, I suppose you might still have picked up some

useful information while you were on your back for one of them." Bright seemed completely oblivious to my inner turmoil—not that I thought he would care one iota, even if he noticed. "I don't suppose they ever showed you who they are beneath the mask?"

Again, I shook my head and bit my lip. I might know who The Shade was masquerading as, but even if I wasn't more than a bit of fun for him, I wasn't going to help Bright anymore than I had to.

"Eh, it was a long shot, but you never know. They do say human women are curious. You never snuck a peak while they were sleeping?"

"They never stayed the night," I muttered and looked down at the floor. The Shade had, though. He had lain underneath me with his arms wrapped around me until dawn when I had asked him to. A small sprout of something akin to hope reared its head from the gloomy cover of despair. He didn't have to do that, but he did it anyway.

Maybe, just maybe, all wasn't lost? I glanced up from beneath my lowered lashes to look at my kidnapper. He regarded me with cold, arrogant eyes, his opinion of worthless humans written all over his expression. He didn't think I stood a chance against him, and maybe he was right, but I was going to do what I could to ensure that he'd never get what he wanted from me. I might just be a chubby human girl, but I wasn't going to give up Lightning or even The Shade to him. And no amount of superpowers would change that.

"Figures," he sighed. "Any marks? Something that made them stand out?"

"You mean, like a tattoo?" I asked, trying my best to look

scared and cowed. Not that that was too hard to achieve just then.

His eyes brightened. "Yes, exactly like a tattoo. Did you see anything like that on either of them?"

I resisted the urge to tell him that Lightning had a really big dolphin tattoo above his pubic region. As much as I would delight in that becoming a circulating rumor in the supe world, I needed any lies I told to be believable.

"Well..." I hesitated.

"Yes?" Bright snapped, obviously impatient to hear about anything that would help him identify his enemies. "Go on."

"The Shade has a sort of cross-shaped scar above his right nipple. And Lightning... Well, he has a really wonky penis." I didn't have to fake a blush when I said that.

"Wonky?" An amused smirk ghosted over the villain's face. "Wonky how, exactly?"

I held up a bent finger for demonstration. "It sorta curves, like this." There. It wasn't a dolphin tattoo, but I had a moment's worth of childish satisfaction regardless.

"I see. What about likes and dislikes? Anything specific?"

I blinked, genuinely confused. "What, like favorite foods?"

Bright shrugged. "Favorite foods, certain phrases you've heard them say a lot, things they like to say or do in bed?"

My face heated up even further. How on earth did he plan on identifying them from what they liked in bed? I nibbled my bottom lip, pretending like I was trying to remember.

"Lightning called me Kittykat sometimes." He'd done that at the Mayor's Ball as well, so I figured I might earn some honesty points by mentioning something he might already know. "But we didn't talk much."

"And when you weren't talking?" he insisted.

I fidgeted a bit on the bed, feeling pretty uncomfortable about talking about my intimate relationship with the two men, even if I was making up the details. "Uhm... They both like a finger up their butts?" It came out as a question, but Bright was too busy snorting with contempt to notice.

"They let a human penetrate them? That's grotesque," he sneered. I wasn't sure if what he found repulsive was the finger comment, or that they supposedly let a human be in a dominant position.

Somewhat spurred on by his easy acceptance of my lies —and, I'll admit, a certain measure of revenge from what they'd both put me through—I continued.

"The Shade moans really loud when he comes, sort of like a cat in pain, and Lightning... well, he..." I resisted the urge to tell my captor that he didn't last long, "likes a lot of foreplay. Like, a weird amount. I'm sorry, I don't know them that well. I would tell you if I knew more—I don't want to die." At least the last part of that sentence was one hundred percent honest, and my sincerity must have shined through, because Bright only grunted instead of pressing for more information.

"Well, thank you, Kathryn, for your cooperation." He sent me a sickly smile. "And for reminding me to never let a human get close. I would love to know what possessed those two to forget what happens if you show any sign of weakness in our society. Leaving a stupid little girl with any sort of knowledge about them to roam around on her own? Big, big mistake. I'm sure you agree."

I ignored the insult to my intelligence and dug my nails

into my palms to brave the question I desperately needed the answer for.

"What happens if one of them does come for me?"

Bright snorted. "Don't get your hopes up. Firstly, they would have to declare—for everyone to hear—that they share a bonded human with their archenemy. The humiliation would be enough to damage their standing in our society, and trust me—no human is worth that.

"Secondly, even if you did mean enough for them to suffer the humiliation, displaying that to every one of their peers would expose that *you* are their weakness. If they come for you, everyone will know exactly how to break them. You wouldn't live long anyway, unless they stuck to you like glue twenty-four-seven.

"But let's pretend for just a moment that either man was, indeed, willing to sacrifice everything for a measly, insignificant human such as yourself. Since it's a double-mark, they would both have to show up to claim you. Together. I don't know how much you know about their strife, but even you must have an inkling about just how much they hate each other. There is nothing and no one that will ever get them to work together. So no, Kathryn. They won't be coming for you. The sooner you accept that, the sooner you'll realize that *I* am all the hope you have left in this world. So if any of what you have told me was a lie... well, let's just say that it's going to be very, very unpleasant to be you."

I stared blankly at him as he got off the chair, gave me an arrogant smirk, and then walked out the door, shutting it behind him with a heavy thud.

He was right. No matter what I might have felt while in their arms—no matter that The Shade had held me through the night or that Lightning had felt possessive enough to reclaim me once he saw his enemy's mark on my neck... There was nothing in this world that would bring the two of them to work together. Especially not the idiotic human who had been stupid enough to fall for them, just because they showed her affection.

Somehow, while gasping from the pain as my heart broke into a million pieces, I recognized the irony of falling for not one, but two unobtainable men—at the same damn time.

THREE

I couldn't see anything for the blindfold covering my eyes, but I could hear just fine. The many voices chattering all around me as Bright led me by a harsh grip on my arm made me try to pull my t-shirt further down in a futile attempt to cover my thighs for these strangers' eyes. I was still wearing the same panties and top I had been when Bright kidnapped me, and he hadn't let me shower or even brush my hair before he'd blindfolded me, pulled me out of my cell and into a car. I felt naked and exposed, and the knowledge that there was no escape for me hadn't brought a blessed numbness to soothe the fear. No, as I stumbled along cold, hard concrete on bare feet, I knew every step brought me closer to my eventual death—and I was scared.

I'd watched enough TV to know that, when there's nothing left to do to save yourself, the only noble way of going out is to face your death calmly, chin raised. I wished with all my heart that I could have been that brave, that strong, but I wasn't. All I managed to do was to refrain from screaming and pleading with my captor as he pulled me alongside him, and that was only because I knew it would yield me nothing but more pain. Bright had made it plenty clear what would happen if I resisted in any way, shape, or form, and I didn't want to make my already dire situation any worse.

Bright stopped without warning, making me stumble forward a step before he yanked me back up, careless of the bruise blooming on my arm beneath his fingers.

"Stay still," he said, his tone not brokering any argument. With a hard yank that pulled my hair, he ripped the blindfold down so it settled around my neck and stepped away.

I blinked against the sudden light, but any relief I felt from finally being free of the blindfold vanished when my eyes regained their focus and I saw my surroundings.

I was in a big, industrial hall of some sort, with metal scaffold lining all the walls from floor to ceiling. And on those scaffolds, and perched on rafters underneath the ceiling, sat more than a hundred masked men and women.

Some were still chatting with whoever was next to them, but the noise slowly died down as more and more quieted, their shining, blue eyes locked on the center of the warehouse. On me.

If I could have, I would have hidden from their unnerving attention, but there was nowhere to go and nothing to hide behind. I curled in on myself and wrapped my arms around my midriff in search of any comfort I could find. It didn't help much.

"Brethren, settle, if you please," a booming voice sounded from behind me. I jolted and snapped my head around, only to see five superhumans sat behind me at what looked like rostrums. One of them was Bright.

The warehouse quieted, until finally, everyone was

completely silent and I could hear my ragged breathing all too clearly as I cowered in the center.

"Bright brings before us a curious discovery," a woman from the rostrums behind me said. "A human carrying a double mark."

Murmurs arose from the scaffolds, and someone shouted, "Whose is she?"

"She belongs to Lightning and The Shade." I could practically hear the malicious smirk in Bright's voice.

The murmurs abruptly crescendoed, turning into shouts of disbelief and raw laughter.

"*Silence!*" the woman from before roared behind me. The warehouse fell silent in an instant. "Is this some kind of a joke, Bright?"

"I assure you, it's not. Go ahead, Whisper, check the girl's neck for yourself. Confirm for everyone who owns this human."

I clenched my teeth at the humiliation of being talked about as if I was nothing more than livestock at an auction, and winced when a hand grabbed my hair and pulled my head to the side. Whoever this Whisper person was, she obviously didn't give one iota whether she hurt me or not.

"Oh, my," she murmured, skimming a gloved finger over my mark. It flared and itched under the stranger's touch, and I flinched in an attempt to get away.

Whisper let go of my hair and returned to her seat.

"Bright is correct. She belongs to both Lightning and The Shade." Her voice echoed through the warehouse, and another murmur went through the gathered superhumans.

"Which begs the question—why the *fuck* is she being paraded around like some pony at a country fair?" The annoyed voice came from my immediate right and I snapped my head around just in time to see Lightning come stalking from the far corner with long, angry strides.

I gaped in astonishment as he made his way toward me. He paused in front of me, but didn't catch my gaze. Instead, he grabbed my right arm and let his fingers skim over the sore place Bright had held while he dragged me from the car. "And why has one of our leaders taken it upon himself to break one of our founding laws by coming into *my* human's home and *kidnapping* her? And borderline mistreating her, from the looks of things. Council, this man," he let go of my arm and pointed at Bright, "took what was mine and left a note *demanding* that I come here to claim it back. Does the law no longer apply to Council members? Because if it does, Bright has certainly broken it, and I insist he be punished for his actions."

Bright banged both hands against the dais and barked a sharp laugh. "You have balls, young one, I'll give you that. But it is not I who need to explain myself this evening. I did not kidnap your little human—I merely ensured the Council got a chance to see this extraordinary claiming mark. Naturally, I had to bring her with me. I'm sure the Council will agree, verifying the existence of a double mark warrants temporarily sequestering the girl."

The four other masked people sitting in the middle of the warehouse murmured in agreement.

Lightning narrowed his eyes into slits. "You have seen her mark. Now, I will be taking her home." This time, his fingers closed around my arm below the bruise, and his touch —even if obscured by the gloves—sent a flood of relief through me so strong my knees nearly buckled. He was here —I was no longer alone in this nightmare.

"Not so fast." Bright raised a hand. "Granted, this is a

unique occurrence, but... I do believe the girl belongs to you *and* The Shade. The Council can't just let you leave with another man's property. Unless, of course, you want to cut her in half, she stays right here."

I glanced up at Lightning, hoping against all hope that he had some sort of a plan. Surely, he wouldn't have come here if he didn't.

Despite my inner speech of reassurance, my stomach did an unpleasant flip-flop at the cold calculation behind Bright's hard eyes. That was the look of a man who knew he'd won.

Lightning gritted his teeth. "Fine. If you're really that desperate to best me, have it your way."

For an awful, heartbreaking moment, I thought he gave me up. I turned to look at him, no longer able to keep my tears at bay, but the short glance he spared me was neither bitter nor indifferent. It was the gentlest of looks, and for that brief moment our eyes met, reassurance cut through my despair. *He wasn't leaving.*

A startled whisper cut through the warehouse, like the rustle of leaves on a breezy autumn day. In front of us, Bright went rigid, and his eyes widened behind the mask. The four other council members shared his expression of stunned disbelief.

"I am here to claim my human." The deep voice was quiet, yet seemed to cut through the hushed whispers like a knife. A large, heavy hand landed on my shoulder opposite of the arm Lightning had a hold of. When I looked up, an all too familiar, black-clad figure loomed by my side.

The Shade had come. He had actually come.

"You... acknowledge her?" Whisper breathed.

He leveled a withering glare at her. "That's what I said."

"This charade ends now." Lightning's voice was cool

steel where The Shade's carried an undercurrent of fire. "We are here, we acknowledge our dual claim. We are *leaving.*"

The tension in the air around me was heavy as a thundercloud, and I could practically feel electric sparks crackle against my skin. Both Lightning and The Shade were tense, shoulders flexed and jaws gritted as if they expected a fight.

"Well, you are certainly in your right." Bright seemed like he'd recouped. He looked from one man to the other with a calculating gaze. "And the Council thanks you for showing us that a dual marking of a human is, indeed, possible. More information of our condition is always invaluable, even if the circumstances may seem... puzzling. But surely, neither of you *wanted* a double claim? How about we let you two fight it out, right here, right now? Whoever kills the other gets full ownership of the girl."

A long, pregnant silence followed his question, and I glanced up at my two protectors in confusion. Surely, they would want to get out of there as soon as possible and leave this awful warehouse behind?

One look at Lightning's narrowed eyes made me reconsider my assumption. I gulped, completely taken aback by the pure hatred I saw there. He was staring at The Shade, shoulders flexing with restraint, as if he actually considered the idea of a fight to the death with his archenemy. Sure, I knew they hated each other—their rivalry was the cause of much speculation on the Internet and even in newspapers—but to let it cloud their judgment enough that they fell headfirst into whatever trap Bright was trying to set for them? That shocked me.

I whipped around to The Shade in hopes of finding more reason there, but he was staring at Lightning with dark determination.

Just awesome.

"Please, I just want to go home," I said, quiet enough that no one else would hopefully hear, hoping against all odds that it would be enough to pull them out of their seemingly overwhelming urge to rip into each other. "Please don't do this now."

The Shade's gaze snapped from Lightning's down to mine, and it was as if some of the grim resolve softened behind his blue eyes. He glanced back up at the other man and then nodded shortly. When I looked to Lightning, his jaw was still so tense his teeth had to be gritted, but he gave my arm a short, reassuring squeeze.

"We have no interest in fighting for your amusement, Bright," The Shade spat. "And we are leaving *now*. One more attempt at stopping us and you will see just how well we can work together if we need to."

Bright looked like he was about to object, an angry slant to his mouth and irritation brewing behind his cold eyes, but Whisper interrupted whatever he was about to say.

"There is no need for threats, Shade. You may take your human and leave. The Council has other matters to discuss that are not suited for human ears. Make sure you blindfold her first. We do not want any of them running their mouths about our meeting grounds. Before you leave, though. I am curious as to *how* you managed to layer her mark?"

"I am not inclined to share that information," Lightning snapped. He grabbed the blindfold around my neck and lifted it, stroking my cheek apologetically with a thumb as he covered my eyes. "As far as I'm concerned, this *meeting* has been a gross misconduct by one of our leaders. I will think long and hard before I volunteer my support for the Council again. Do not ask me any favors."

"As upset as you may be, I am asking for information that could lead to a better understanding of our race. Whatever grudge you have with Bright shouldn't affect your allegiance to our society." Even though I couldn't see Whisper from my dark world behind the blindfold, I could hear the frustration in her clipped voice loud and clear. For whatever reason, she seemed genuinely interested in the cause of the double mark, where Bright had been more interested in how he could use this information against the two.

"You should have thought about that before you white-washed this kidnapping of our human for the benefit of your fellow Council member." The snarl came from my other side —from The Shade. "We owe you nothing. Count yourself lucky this is all the repercussion you get."

Strong arms grabbed me tight and hoisted me up against a muscular chest. I managed to bite down on my shriek of surprise, but when the air around me erupted in a loud *crack* and an unpleasant sensation of being yanked backwards by my navel followed, I lost the fight. I screamed and clung to whoever was carrying me as icy mist closed around my body, wrapping chilling tendrils around my naked skin.

FOUR

"Shh, you're okay." The shushing was accompanied by a quick kiss on my lips that snapped me out of it as effectively as a bucket of water would have.

A faint crack from close by us made me jerk and fumble with the blindfold, but the growling voice that accompanied it belonged to The Shade.

"Give her to me."

The strong arms around me—Lightning's arms—clutched me tighter. "If you want her, you'll have to take her."

I managed to pull the blindfold down just in time to see The Shade's dark figure step right up against me, close enough for his wide chest to brush against my body. "That can easily be arranged."

It was at that point the many sensory impressions since I'd gotten kidnapped finally caught up to me. All the fear, humiliation, degradation, heartbreak, pain and desperate hope crashed together in my overworked mind in one, insurmountable tangle of emotion. Without warning, I started to cry.

It wasn't the cute, dainty "a few, glistening tears and a sniffle" sort of crying either. It was open-mouthed, snot-spewing ugly-crying.

"Now look what you've done!" Lightning snarled. "Shh, baby, you're safe now. It's over, I promise. Stop crying." The last part sounded just a little desperate.

I hiccuped in an attempt at obeying, but the tears kept coming, now that the floodgates had opened. It was such a relief to finally let go of all the tension that my brain seemed completely incapable of keeping itself together. I was safe—against all odds, they had come for me, and I was safe. Despite Bright's threats and my own lack of trust in the two men who had claimed me as their own, despite the fact that I didn't know what would happen now that Lightning and The Shade had shown every supe in the city that I was their weakness, I knew I was safe, at least for a little while. And right now, it was enough.

The Shade stroked a large hand through my hair. "She needs the comfort of her own home. Bring her there. But, if you teleport on me again, I *am* taking you down."

Lightning snorted derisively. "You mean you would try."

Despite his argumentative tone, he didn't do the thing that had felt like being pulled backwards by my navel again —*teleporting*. *Christ*. Instead, he shifted me in his grip so I could wrap my legs around his hips and my arms around his shoulders.

"Hang on tight, Kittykat. And don't look down while we move, mmkay? I don't want you to barf."

I obviously looked down the second he set off, leaping into the night.

"Oh my Gooood!" My shrill shriek pitched into a long, drawn-out scream as we dropped toward the ground at nerve wracking speed. But before we impacted, Lightning grabbed a pylon with the hand he didn't have around my waist and swung us back up into the air, propelling us forward.

I recognized the dark, abandoned buildings of the industrial quarter behind us before I clenched my eyes firmly shut and dug my fingernails into the back of Lightning's suit, determined not to watch the rest of what felt like an unhinged amusement ride. It didn't stop me from feeling the sudden drops, nor my stomach from lurching dangerously each time Lightning changed altitude with a powerful leap, and I screamed nonstop the entire way home. At least I was too preoccupied to continue crying.

When the wild motions finally halted, it took me several moments to brave opening my eyes.

I blinked into the darkness, the warmer air against my skin along with the now faded sounds from the city making me realize that we were inside. The faint, familiar scent of my own apartment made my iron-locked muscles release their death grip on Lightning as they practically jellified. I slid down his strong body until I landed on my feet with a thump, and would have fallen straight on my butt if he hadn't supported my weight.

I was home.

"Don't start crying again." The note of panic in Lightning's voice made me bite my trembling lip. Right. No more crying. I'd played the role of a damsel in distress enough for a lifetime tonight, and if there was anything I desperately needed right now, it was finding my own strength again, after having been treated like I was nothing more than an item.

That, and food. Bright hadn't exactly bothered to keep me fed.

I stepped back from Lightning's embrace, gingerly testing my legs' strength and finding that I could hold my own weight.

"Kathryn..."

I held up a hand, silencing the superhuman. "Not now. I need to eat something, and then I need to sleep."

"We need to talk—"

"I don't want to talk!" I snapped. Unexpected anger rushed through me and pounded in my temples. Irritably, I rubbed at them and stalked to the fridge. He—and The Shade—had saved me, I knew that, and yet my suddenly flaring temper had me itching to lash out at him. What I needed was to get my blood sugar up. "I want to *eat* and *sleep*. And if you're still around in the morning, then we can talk."

I ripped open the fridge door, hoping my dig at his abandonment had gone through loud and clear. However thankful I was for them showing up to save my ass, it didn't change the hurtful things he'd said before leaving me after having slept with me. Nor the fact that all this supernatural crap I'd face-planted in was all thanks to him and The Shade.

I grabbed some cold cuts, cheese, mayo and lettuce and slammed the door shut instead of giving voice to my—possibly unreasonable—anger. I was midway through sandwich making when The Shade swung in through my kitchen window as easily as had it been a wide open door.

"Jesus Christ!" I snapped when I dropped the knife I'd used to spread mayonnaise onto my sandwich with a loud clank. "Stop doing that!"

"Kitten—"

"*I am not your fucking kitten!*" I whipped around to glare at him, fists clenched at my sides. "I am not a thing, I am not your property, and I am not a weak baby animal! I am a human being, I am an actual *person,* and right now, you need to not speak to me!"

Okay, so maybe it wasn't the best way ever to thank the men who had just faced off against their own kind to ensure I lived to see another day, but all I needed at that moment was to not be reminded of the terrible, humiliating Council meeting and Bright's invasive questioning.

The Shade grunted, and I was pretty sure no one ever spoke to him like that—at least, no one who got to live. Right then, I didn't care.

I turned back around to stare at my half-made sandwich. My hands were shaking so bad I couldn't even put the bread on top of the ham.

Strong, muscled arms slipped around me from the back, steading my trembling body. Lightning pressed his head lightly against mine until my body slowly relaxed, surrendering to his soothing scent and warm presence. I was still angry, but the fight seeped out of me with every calming breath he exhaled against my ear.

The Shade moved from the window with feline grace, bent to sweep up the knife I'd dropped on the floor and proceeded to assemble my triple-decker sandwich with measured, precise movements that resembled the ease with which he handled his swords. The thought of The Shade spending time in a kitchen on a regular basis, making sandwiches, made a helpless little giggle burst out.

Lightning kissed my temple and lifted me up. I thought about protesting, but my limbs felt too weak to keep me upright anyway. He carried me to my sofa and plopped me down before wrapping a blanket around my shoulders. The Shade placed a plate with the sandwich on the table in front of me, and ghosted his lips over the top of my head.

I glanced up at the two superhumans, who were both watching me intently from opposite ends of my designated living room area. It possibly should have felt intrusive to be stared at like an animal at the zoo while I was eating, but it didn't. It felt... oddly comforting.

I didn't bother to try and work out why, and instead grabbed for my sandwich. My stomach growled appreciatively, and I think I moaned around the first, delicious bite. I didn't look up again before I'd eaten the entire thing and a pleasant lethargy overtook my body and brain.

I MUST HAVE FALLEN ASLEEP, because when I opened my eyes, daylight filtered in through the windows, illuminating my apartment.

I was on my back on the sofa, and someone had pulled my only surviving blanket up around my body. Who knew supes could be so... *cuddly*.

Yawning, I sat up and stretched, cringing at my sore muscles. It wasn't like I'd done any strenuous activities, but my body felt like it'd been through a meat grinder.

"Feeling better?"

The calm voice cutting through the silence made me jolt in surprise and look in the direction of the speaker. Lightning sat on the other side in my armchair, stretched back with his boots on my coffee table. The Shade was perched on my office chair, arms folded over his chest like a great, looming shadow against the gray light from the rainy day visible through the windows.

I don't know if I'd expected them to leave or not, but it was still pretty odd to wake up to both of them just hanging out in my home while I'd been fast asleep.

"Yeah. Thanks. I need a shower, though."

I did feel better—as in, not on the verge of either tears or angry outbursts. Instead, I felt grimy and gross from not having had a change of clothes or a shower, and mildly ashamed at how I'd treated the two men who had risked everything to save me.

"I'm... I'm sorry about yelling at you," I said, glancing from Lightning to The Shade. ""I didn't... Thank you."

"Go shower." The Shade nodded toward my bathroom with his chin. "We'll talk after."

THE WATER WAS a blessing against my skin, washing away not only the sweat and dirty of the past few days, but also helping me clear my head. As scary as last night—and the time spent as Bright's prisoner—had been, it wasn't time to be a fainting little virgin who couldn't handle herself. More than ever, Bright needed to be stopped, and I quite possibly had the key somewhere in the files I'd taken pictures of in the mayor's office.

And then there was The Shade and Lightning.

My stomach did a flip-flop at the thought of my two lovers. Against all odds, they had come for me, humiliating themselves in the eyes of their peers and even managing to put their differences aside to save me. That had to mean something—it had to mean that, whatever it was I felt about them, it wasn't completely unrequited.

Warmth blossomed in my chest, even though a small, pragmatic voice at the back of my mind reminded me that if that was the case, there were entirely different issues to deal with—like the fact that there were two of them, and one of me, for starters.

My pussy clenched unexpectedly, and heat flushed my cheeks at its unwelcomed input. There was no way those two would be okay with sharing me, and I needed to get my mind completely out of the gutter—there were much more important things to consider, other than their sexy bodies and thick cocks.

My nipples tightened with arousal at the memory of the feel of their hard lengths inside of me... *Dammit!*

I turned the shower on ice cold and forced myself to remain under the freezing spray until all thoughts of sex were gone.

Then I hurried out of the shower so I could start toweling myself warm again. The fact of the matter was that neither man was particularly great boyfriend material. Lightning had made it plenty clear he wasn't looking for any sort of romantic connection, and he was a bit of a jerk to boot, and The Shade... I bit my lip, hard, when I recalled "Shaw Industries" noted down next to the funding of the blueprints for the scary-looking weapon in the mayor's files. The Shade was most definitely not a good guy.

Right. So that had to be my priority. Warm, fuzzy feelings would have to wait until I knew just how much of a threat The Shade was to me, to Lightning, and to the city. But I couldn't reveal that I knew his identity—no matter what had made him come get me at the Council meeting, I had no delusions of the length of my lifespan if he got so much as a hint that I knew who he was. Which, by the way, wasn't really something to build a relationship on.

Wait, relationship? Okay, someone clearly needed a reality check, pronto. No one had said anything about relationships. They had, however, called me "theirs" on numerous occasions, which didn't equate to love. Affection, sure. I couldn't really argue against that, after what they'd both done for me, but people with pets were usually also quite fond of them. Didn't mean they were in a relationship with their dog. Or *kitten*.

I finished getting dressed and made my way back to where my two, sexy problems waited, mouth set in a grim line.

"We need to talk," I said as I sat back down on the sofa, arms folded across my chest.

"Yes, we do." Lightning glanced darkly at The Shade for a moment, before returning his gaze to me. "You need to be kept somewhere safe, Kathryn. Somewhere no supe will find you. I have a couple of safe houses—"

I opened my mouth to cut him off, ready to tell him exactly what I thought about being "kept somewhere," but The Shade beat me to it.

"She is not going to any of your 'safe houses.' *I* will hide her in one of *my* safe locations." It was a low growl, and I could have sworn he was flexing his muscles in some primitive display of strength.

"The fuck you will." Lightning's hands tightened around the armrests on his chair. "There is no chance in hell I'm letting a glorified pickpocket take off with *my* woman. She is under *my* protection—she stays at *my* safe house.

"She's under my protection too, you fool," The Shade

growled. "And I trust you to not steal her from me as much as I trust Bright's good intentions."

Jesus Christ. This was getting more and more infuriating by the minute.

"That's enough! You both need to stop this crap right now!"

Both supes' heads snapped towards me, their unnerving eyes locking on mine. I felt some of my gusto-brought-on-by-irritation fade at the sheer weight of their joined attention, but gave myself a mental shake. Now was not the time to get all self-conscious and wet-pantied.

"I have had enough of being treated like something you own. I get that you've got different ways of doing things than the rest of us, but *I* am *human*. And I'm not going to be some prize you fight over. Got that?"

Neither answered. I took that as consent.

"And before either of you go any further with this whole macho competition you've got going on, *we*," I gestured between them and myself, "need to talk. I am very thankful you didn't leave me to get murdered by Bright, don't get me wrong here, but that leaves the question as to why?"

They both looked at me as if they were questioning my mental capacity.

"You're ours," Lightning said, speaking slowly and carefully. "We will protect you at any cost. I thought I'd made that perfectly clear."

I blushed as warmth spread from my chest at the memory of how he'd declared he'd protect me "with his own flesh," if need be, before taking me to bed. Then I recalled what he'd said *after* the sex, and my blood cooled significantly.

"Yeah? I also remember you saying that you weren't my

boyfriend, and that you made it more than clear that you have no feelings for me. You know, *after* you got into my pants. And according to Bright, coming to get me together like you did was supposed to be the ultimate humiliation—in fact, he seemed pretty damn convinced that there was no chance in hell you'd show up. So excuse me for being just a little bit confused."

The way Lightning's eyes darkened, I was pretty certain he was frowning behind his mask. "It's not that simple. The mark..."

The fucking mark again. I threw up my hands in disgust. "Great! So you're spellbound to sacrifice life and reputation by a mark you put on my neck even though you'd rather not, and I can't keep my thighs together because of it. Marvelous! And I take it it's the same for you?" I leveled an annoyed glare at The Shade.

His scarred lip pulled up, either in amusement or annoyance. "Not exactly. I have no ambivalent emotions when it comes to you, kitten. I don't know why the mark influences me as it does, but I am smart enough to go with it when my magic calls out like it does for you. You will be by my side by the end of this, no matter the cost."

Great. I paled a little as I looked into his determined gaze, realizing just how seriously he meant it. And that, despite some traitorous parts of my body heating pleasantly at that realization, being by The Shade's side—*no matter the cost*—didn't promise any other emotion than possessiveness, nor did it spell out a future that I got any say in. Especially not considering the photo on my phone taunting me with its existence.

I glanced at Lightning, who was glaring daggers at The Shade. He needed to know—and the sooner, the better.

"Right. Well, what girl hasn't dreamed of those words? 'Magic made me do it.' Christ." I scrubbed my face with both hands and took a deep breath to clear my head. There were more important things to worry about than my wounded ego and confusing feelings-that-shouldn't-even-exist. "Maybe we better start focusing on Bright and how we can unravel this mess instead."

The Shade narrowed his eyes at me as Lightning pressed his lips into a firm, disapproving line.

"*We* are not going to sort anything. *You* are going to stay far, far away from this mess, and *I* will sort it out. Lightning too, if he gets his head out of his ass. But not you."

I stared up at him, gobsmacked. "Excuse me? I'm the one who just got kidnapped! I think I'm entitled to a bigger role than virginal sacrifice here!"

Lightning snorted behind me. "Yeah, not happening, Kittykat. No more sneaking around the mayor's office and sticking your nose into things that can get you into trouble. And for the record, there's nothing 'virginal' about you."

Perfect. The one thing they *could* agree on would of course have to be treating me like an incompetent doll.

"It's not like I want to dive headfirst into the next supervillain's net, I promise," I sighed, stepping back a little now that they didn't seem like they were about to rip into each other at any moment. "But, quite honestly, I don't think you two have any clue where to begin looking, or you would have done something by now. I do."

Lightning's eyes narrowed to slits. "This wouldn't happen to have anything to do with what you specifically said you *didn't* find in Wilkins' office, would it?"

"You were snooping around in Wilkins' office? After I *ordered* you not to investigate anymore? *Twice!*"

I ignored The Shade's incensed interruption and went over to my computer. My phone was still safely hidden away behind it. I fished it out and scrolled through my images, heart pounding in my throat.

"I found blueprints of a large weapon that looks an awful lot like Bright's gun—the one he used in a bank robbery last December. And I found a linked payment to it as well." I held out my phone to them both, eyes fixed on The Shade. "It came from Shaw Industries."

FIVE

The Shade's expression didn't change as he stared at my phone's screen, but his posture tensed up just enough for my throat to tighten.

"That's impossible," he murmured. "Elias Shaw isn't involved with the mayor—or Bright."

"No, he's not," Lightning said.

I finally took my eyes off The Shade to look at him, eyebrows raised in confusion. "It says right here, though. Do you think the mayor's just using Shaw Industries as a cover name for someone else?"

"Nah, it's Shaw Industries, all right. But Elias doesn't know what's going on. He's got someone on the inside funneling money to a few illicit activities and hiding the trail. I've been keeping tabs on his board for a few weeks, but no one's coming up as suspicious."

The Shade looked about as surprised as I felt. "*You've* been trying to flush out a mole in Shaw's business? Aren't the unwashed masses at the bottom of society more your game?"

Lightning scoffed. "I don't give a shit what income level the people I help are on. Not that I expect a lousy pickpocket to understand that."

"Says the glorified action figure. But let's get back on point, shall we? Someone's funneling funds from an unsuspecting CEO into the mayor's account—which was then used to build that nasty gun Bright likes to flash around? Have I got that right?" The Shade looked from me to Lightning.

I nodded, frowning at my phone. If Lightning was correct—and I had no reason to believe he would lie about something like that—then Elias Shaw wasn't on the mayor's side. My mark throbbed in a very *"I told you so"* manner that made my nipples harden. I rubbed distractedly at it until it settled down to a pleasant tingle, and cast a shy glance at The Shade.

When Elias had asked for my phone number, he'd given me his in return, mentioning something about a coffee date. While mulling over my complicated tangle of emotions when it came to the two supes, I'd disregarded it as some convoluted ploy from his side that I just couldn't work out. But if he really wasn't on the mayor's payroll, then... then maybe it had really just been... a date.

Maybe, despite his threatening persona and promises of "keeping me by his side," like I was some trinket, his interest in me was genuine?

Warmth fluttered in my belly, and for a few, euphoric moments, I allowed myself to imagine what it would be like to be truly loved by someone so powerful and intense. Then I looked at Lightning, and the happiness died down, only to be replaced by heartache. Why, *why*, did I want him so bad, when he'd made it clear his only interest in me stemmed from the mark? Was it really just the magic they'd talked about? And was that the reason that I couldn't be fully happy with the thought of just one of them truly caring for me?

It was preposterous, of course, no matter the reason. I'd never expected any man who could provoke the response in my heart and body as either of them did to take an interest in me—and I'd made my peace with that. And now... now, my greedy heart would not be satisfied with anything but both of them.

I might as well start looking into getting a load of cats.

"You need to show me everything you've found." The Shade's voice ripped me out of my depressed musings, and I flinched as cool anger flickered through Lightning's glowing eyes at the demand.

"I *need* to show you exactly nothing, Shade," he sneered. "If you want to find out what's going on in some billionaire's dealings, I'm sure you can torture a person or two to figure it out on your own."

"Maybe I will," The Shade growled. "How many would it take for you to get the stick out of your ass?"

I pinched the bridge of my nose. Getting them to work together to defeat Bright was going to be enough of a challenge. Turning my half-baked dreams of being with both of them into any sort of reality just wasn't going to happen, and the sooner I made my peace with that, the better.

"Look, you're both investigating the mayor and Bright, and you need to work together to stop whatever he's doing. I don't know why you two hate each other so much, but if you were able to put it aside to get me, you can put it aside to fight a common enemy, right?"

The Shade pursed his lips, an unhappy draw to them.

"She is not incorrect. We can't let him live, after how he took her. If we kill him, it should give others pause before they try the same stunt. But neither of us can do that on our own, or he would be long dead."

"That's easy for you to say," Lightning growled. He got up from the armchair in one, graceful movement and rolled his shoulders, as if the mere subject of working together had made them tense. "I have zero guarantee that you won't align with Bright midway through, and I'm not risking her life on that."

Anger blazed through The Shade's eyes. He ripped out of the chair and stopped right in front of Lightning a second later, teeth bared and muscles tensed. "Don't you *dare* insinuate that I would betray her. You were the one who left her alone and crying, not me."

Something oddly reminiscent of *guilt* flashed in Lightning's eyes, but was quickly replaced by hatred. "Do not turn this on me, Shade. You have pulled that stunt before, remember? People died because of your changing allegiance."

"Our past has nothing to do with this. Are you really willing to risk Kathryn over an old grudge? Because if that's the case, I am not the one who is a danger here, and I won't hesitate to eliminate you if you pose a threat to her."

"Uh, guys." I got up from the sofa and carefully wedged myself in between the two superhumans, who were squaring up against each other, teeth bared and bodies tensed. The energy in the room was practically electric, making nervous jolts travel along my scalp and down my spine. To say that things had gotten tense would be an understatement. "Let's calm down, okay? We're not going to get anything sorted if you two are at each other's throats."

A low growl rumbled out of The Shade's chest, but at

least they didn't launch at each other. I took that as my cue to continue.

"Look, we need to figure out why the mayor is bankrolling Bright's gun, and if there's more between them than that. I only found the blueprints for that gun, and the connection to Shaw Industries in the documents I took pictures of. Is there someone within the supe community that you trust, who might know something?"

"You don't ask those kinds of questions in our society," Lightning grunted, though his eyes were fixed on the far wall as if he was going through possible contacts as he spoke. "Of course, you don't steal someone's bonded human, either, so maybe it's about time we set aside any pretense of following the rules."

"With the evidence Kathryn found that Bright's relying on the mayor for funding, we should have enough to prove that he's unfit for leadership, at least," The Shade mumbled. He, too, had gotten a far-away look in his eyes, as if he was mulling over the possibilities. "That's direct involvement of a human in supe affairs."

"We need more than a paper trail," Lightning sighed. "We need something flashier, and you know he's involved in something dirtier than that. Why would he risk exposure by involving the mayor?"

"Can't you just kidnap him?"

Both supes turned their heads toward me with a snap, and I faltered under their incredulous stares. "I mean... the mayor? To question him?"

The Shade's face split in a surprised grin. "The kitten shows her claws."

Lightning grimaced. "As endearing as I find your descent into a criminal mindset, we can't just kidnap a man as important as the mayor. If we do, and don't kill him, he will undoubtedly be rather negatively set when it comes to supes in general, and that won't end well for anyone. If we *do* kill him... Well, I'm sure The Shade would be all about that, but I'd rather not execute a man just for fiddling with the book-keeping, if that turns out to be all he's done."

I blanched and nodded. I hadn't really thought that one through to its natural conclusion. "All right, no kidnapping. Then what do we do?"

"Mirome."

I looked up at The Shade with both eyebrows raised, but it was Lightning who broke the silence that followed that one word.

"I suppose... if anyone would know, it would be him."

"He knows everything about everyone," The Shade confirmed. "He would be the natural place to go for answers."

"Who's Mirome?" I asked, looking from one man to the other. They both seemed oddly hesitant. "And if he's the local gossip, then what are we waiting for?"

"He's an old friend," Lightning said, his voice quieter than normal. "There is... history there."

I didn't manage to get my suspiciously raised eyebrows back under control, and they shot up high on my forehead. "You *both* have history with this man? The kind that makes you hesitant to ask him questions? Whatever this story is, I want to know."

Neither man answered me, but the tension in the room grew noticeably. *O-okay. Major sore subject-alert?*

Before I could open my mouth to barrage them with questions, a knock on my front door pounded through the loft.

I tensed, cold fear taking an instant hold of my mind as images of running through dark alleys and being dragged out into the night by Bright flashed before my mind's eye in a swirl of terror. It wasn't until then that I realized how much my experiences with the dark side of St. Anthony had marked me.

I didn't even notice I'd reached out to clutch at The Shade's—who stood nearest—arm until he pulled me into a loose embrace and mumbled, " You're safe, kitten. Bad guys don't knock."

"You would know," Lightning muttered. "I take it you're not expecting visitors?"

I shook my head, trying to calm down my racing heart. "No. It's probably just one of the neighbors." Despite my attempt at rational logic, my nails were still dug safely into The Shade's black suit.

It knocked again, more insistently this time, and Lightning sighed. "Right, then. I hope your neighbors are fans."

He walked smoothly to the door, turned the lock and pulled it open.

"Oh, my God!" The breathy gasp from the person blocked from my view by Lightning's bulky mass carried equal measures of sheer shock and excitement. "You're Lightning!"

"Keen observation. And you are?" Lightning's tone had regained its usual measure of sarcasm.

"Oh, sorry! I'm Trish—Kathryn's friend. I need to speak with her, urgently. Is she here?"

SIX

It was almost as if I'd managed to forget, somewhere in the middle of being kidnapped and rescued, that there were other people in this world than superhumans and villainous politicians. The arrival of my friend at my doorstep jerked me out of the scary, dark fear that had haunted me for the past however many days, and into the light. A surge of hope and exhilaration jolted through me, and I wrestled myself out of The Shade's light grasp and practically ran for the door.

"Trish!"

Her face was still a mask of surprise and borderline awe, but it broke into smile when I practically pushed Lightning aside and pulled her into a fierce hug.

"Oh, thank God you're here!"

"That's what I was going to say," she said as she freed herself and glanced at Lightning, who was watching us, arms crossed over his chest and mouth set in a firm line. "I tried calling you all day yesterday, and there was no answer.

Usually, you at least text me back! I was worried. What's going on?"

"Uh..." I looked up at Lightning above my friend's curly, black hair. The warning in his glowing eyes was unmistakable—*tell her nothing*.

But this was Trish, and I needed to talk to her—needed someone who understood how scared I was, without wanting to treat me like an incompetent child.

"You better come in." I stepped aside, ignoring Lightning's quiet hiss at my disobedience. "It's a long story."

She stepped across the threshold, still seemingly unable to take her eyes off Lightning, which was probably why she didn't notice the other supe until the door was safely locked behind her and I directed her attention at him.

"Trish, there's someone else I want you to meet," I said, eying The Shade carefully to gauge his reaction to my friend's sudden arrival. Judging from the way his upper lip curved in a silent snarl, he was probably about as excited as Lightning.

My friend finally managed to rip her gaze from Lightning's narrowed eyes, but when she spotted The Shade's black-clad figure, the smile faded and was replaced with near-comical terror. She made a funny little squeaky noise and stopped so abruptly that I nearly walked straight into her.

"Kat...!"

"Yeah, I know," I said, placing a calming hand on her shoulder. "He's been helping me. He won't hurt you."

"That entirely depends on whether or not I find you a threat," The Shade growled, looking every bit as terrifying as his reputation painted him out to be.

"Oh, stop it!" I snapped. "Trish is my best friend, and I

trust her a hell of a lot more than I do you two. You will do absolutely nothing to her, or so help me, I will make you pay. And that goes for both of you." I didn't exactly have any plan as to how I'd go about making either superhuman *pay*, but it was largely ignored anyway.

"She needs to leave. Now."

I glared at The Shade. "No, she doesn't. You can trust her, and she might be able to help. She's a reporter with DNSA, and I already told her about your first visit, Lightning. She hasn't told anyone, and she won't tell anyone anything else. Right, Trish?"

"Uh-huh." She didn't take her eyes off The Shade, who was staring at her in return, lip still curled in warning.

"Oh, for heaven's sake!" I grabbed her by the arm and began dragging her toward the only room with a door in my loft—the bathroom. "You two—don't kill each other. We'll be back in a bit."

Once the lock clicked behind me and I'd turned on the tap to hopefully block out our voices from any superhuman hearing, Trish visibly relaxed, though her face was still a study in disbelief.

"*Wow*, Kat."

"I know."

"The *Shade?* What the hell's going on?"

I scrubbed my face with both hands, trying to find the words to explain what had happened. "It's all so messed up, Trish. I'm so in over my head. But they've both been helping me—helping me survive. This thing... it's so much deeper than what we ever thought."

Trish looked at me with that same, familiar expression of calm overview, like she had every time I freaked out about college assignments back when we used to share a room. If she hadn't become one of the city's top journalists, she would have been great as an emergency dispatcher. She put her hands on either side of my arms and pressed gently, calming me with her familiar presence. "Just start from the beginning. Tell me everything."

Had it been anyone but Trish, I wouldn't have. At the very least, I would have left out the details about how I'd been *claimed* by both the city's favorite hero and its most feared villain and somehow landed in a bizarre love triangle, only without the love-bit. But this *was* Trish—my best friend, the only one who'd stuck around for more than the occasional social media chat after everyone separated after college. So I told her everything that had happened since the last time we spoke.

"Hold up... you *slept* with *both* of them?"

I flushed, somewhat embarrassed by her scandalized tone. "It just sort of happened, okay. Can we maybe move on to the important part? The one where superhumans are controlling the mayor, and he's funding Bright's weapons?"

"Yeah, okay... you just sort of happened to fall on their penises. And the way you're blushing, like a teenager with her first crush, doesn't mean you're in love with either the man whose bad manners you wrote an entire article about, or the one who's known for terrorizing the city on a regular basis. But fine, if you want to play coy, it's your prerogative. You said a source gave you the idea to look for the files you found at the mayor's office? Who is it?"

I frowned. Surely, there were more important things to worry about than who pointed me in the right direction. "I can't name him—I promised he would be completely anonymous." Ignoring how The Shade had threatened his name out of me, of course. "It doesn't matter, though. What matters is that he was right."

She pinched her full lips and crossed her arms in a pose I knew all too well. With an inward sigh, I steeled myself for a lecture.

"It's my reputation on the line too, Kat. I can't just bring an article based on some anonymous source, without checking it myself. It's Journalism 101."

My cheeks heated again, though this time from annoyance rather than embarrassment. As much as I appreciated her being here for me, I didn't need another reminder of how she was a *real* reporter, and I wasn't—at least, not in the circles she frequented. "It's also Journalism 101 to protect your source in a case as dangerous as this, and honestly—this is so beyond getting a story in the paper, Trish. I was *kidnapped*, for Chrissake! If we are going to get to the bottom of this, we need to work with The Shade and Lightning—not try to chase a story for the front page. I was hoping you would help me figure out what the mayor is up to, so we can uncover exactly what his relationship to Bright is—so maybe, we can avoid getting killed."

Trish's lips were still pinched as she looked at me, and it dawned on me that this was the first time I'd ever really taken a stand against her.

"All right," she finally said. "You've got a point. I'll help as best I can. That's sort of why I was trying to get a hold of you, actually. I know someone who might be able to help."

My temper fizzled, and I felt a minor wave of guilt at my outburst. "Oh, that's great, Trish. Who?"

She grimaced. "It's one of the senior reporters at the station. But he wants to fly under the radar for now, so I can't give you his name yet. But trust me, he's big. He wants to meet with you. Think you can ditch those two and come with me?"

I frowned, worrying my lip between my teeth. "I doubt it. Can't they come, though? They're as keen to figure this mess out as I am."

Trish shook her head decisively. "No, definitely not. He's not... he doesn't trust superhumans in general, that's why he's interested in this case." She glanced at the toilet door. "How about I text you, later, and you can let me know if you're available?"

As in, sneak out when my two self-appointed guards were preoccupied.

I nodded, giving her a thankful smile. As much as I wanted to cling to either supe for protection right now, I needed to get my big girl pants on if I was going to pull my weight in this endeavor. And I couldn't exactly fault Trish's colleague for not wanting to get involved with superhumans, what with my own, recent experience with their world.

"I better get going, then," she said. "I don't think your boyfriends are all that keen on my presence here."

I flinched. "They're not my *boyfriends*."

"Yeah, sure. You do the horizontal mambo with them, and they're hanging around your apartment, flexing their muscles and *protecting* you. Nothing about that sounds like they're boyfriends. No siree! " A wide smirk and her trademark, sparkling eyes had returned, reminding me all too well of the fun, sarcastic girl I'd known in college.

"I think it's time for you to leave!" I said, ushering her toward the closed bathroom door. "Out you go!"

She laughed and unlocked the door, sashaying out of the small room as if she was no longer the least concerned about the two men in the room. I turned off the tap and followed her, pleasantly surprised by the light spark in my chest caused by my friend's banter. Despite how fucked up everything had gotten, I still had a friend like Trish in my corner. Something about that fact made hope that I was going to be okay at the end of this spread through my body.

"Bye, boys!" she said at the two supes waiting by my desk, giving them a cheerful wave. I didn't know exactly when she'd gone from terrified to apparently completely calm around them, but the flippant way she spoke to them made me laugh in amazement. Typical Trish—she could turn any situation around to suit her.

Or... almost any situation.

Trish had nearly made it to the front door, when the air next to her erupted in a dark burst, and The Shade materialized in her path. His big hand clamped around her shoulder, halting her, and what was visible of his face was twisted into an unmistakable threat of violence.

"You get to leave here because Kathryn trusts you, but make no mistake—one word out of you about anything she's told you, or even just that you've seen us here with her, and I *will* kill you. Slowly and painfully. Do you understand? Just one word."

Others would have instantly cowered at The Shade threatening them like that, but Trish glared back at him with obvious defiance. It did, however, crumble somewhat when he bared his teeth at her and growled a low warning—not even Trish could withstand the primal response to such a predatory threat.

She winced, undoubtedly in reaction to the tight grip on her shoulder, and swallowed. "Yeah, okay, I understand. I won't say anything."

The villain glared down at her for a long moment,

driving home his point and power with his burning gaze, before he finally let go. Trish practically ran out the door, not giving us as much as a cursory look before she slammed it shut behind her, leaving me alone with the two supes once again.

"That was really rude," I hissed, putting my hands on my hips and squaring up against the man who had just sent my best friend packing. "Where do you get off, acting like a bully to someone who wants to help me? Help *us*? This is my home, not yours."

He turned to me then, some of the warning still remaining in his blazing, blue eyes. The intensity in them made me gulp involuntarily, and something south of my navel heat up. "Be happy I want to please you enough that I didn't kill her, just for the risk she poses. You swear she's trustworthy, but you could be blinded by your soft feelings and history with her. Did you know DNSA Network is owned by Shaw Industries?"

I scoffed at the ridiculousness of that question. "She's a journalist—she's not our mole."

"She could be working for the mole and not even realize," Lightning—to my utter surprise—interjected. "You can't trust someone just because they call themselves your friend."

"Well, she's not involved with the mole, period. And I would really appreciate it if another time, you didn't go out of your way to try and drive away the only friend I have. I don't particularly want to be all alone in the world—especially not now."

"You're not alone," The Shade said, his voice surprisingly soft. He walked toward me, and I couldn't help but swallow thickly at the quiet smolder in his eyes as he looked at me. "I'm here."

He reached my side and stroked a hand through my hair, tipping my head back enough to lock my gaze with his. My tongue darted out to wet my lips of its own accord when his eyes swept to my mouth.

"*We* are here." Lightning appeared by The Shade's side, his glowing eyes holding no less heat than his enemy's. A gloved hand slipped up underneath my shirt and brushed against my bare hip, raising goosebumps of anticipation along my skin. "You will never be alone."

I wanted to remind Lightning how he'd made it clear he wasn't in it for anything but the magic tying us together via my mark, but the way he looked at me as if I was something precious made my stupid heart flutter in my chest. It was as if they'd spoken some magic spell, because everything that had been tight and scared inside of me, loosened at their words.

Another hand joined the first, trailing up along my soft stomach to cup a breast. My nipple tightened in response, and I moaned softly and reached out to support my suddenly wobbly knees against The Shade's strong body. I didn't think —didn't want to remind myself of all the reasons why I shouldn't allow either man's touch, and most especially not together. It felt so good to just give in and let go of all the fear and doubt for just a moment.

It lasted until someone's—I couldn't tell whose—hand dipped into my panties and brushed over the top of my cleft.

The zing of sharp excitement tore me out of the lethargic haze brought on by their more gentle caresses, and I stumbled backward, nearly tripping over my own legs.

"Ah, w-we should probably not do that," I stammered, while avoiding their heated eyes by fumbling with my clothes in an attempt at straightening them.

"Why not?" The Shade challenged.

I dared a surprised glance up at them. "Um, for starters, you hate each other? And then there's the whole Bright situation. The sooner we get going to meet your friend, the sooner we have a chance at ending this nightmare."

"*We* are not going anywhere, Kittykat." Lightning's smoldering gaze cooled somewhat as he folded his arms across his wide chest. "You and I are staying here while The Shade talks to Mirome. I don't want you mixed up in anymore supe business."

"I think what you meant to say is that *you* will go talk to Mirome while *I* stay here with Kathryn," The Shade growled, narrowing his eyes at his enemy. "I am not leaving you alone with her—we both know you would love nothing more than to take off the second my back's turned."

"Like you would, if I went and you stayed, Again, may I remind you which of us has the better reputation when it comes to honesty?" Lightning stared at him. "It's not like we can leave her on her own, without risking Bright swooping in."

Splendid. Why was it that they seemed perfectly okay with groping me together, while every other form of cooperation was a complete no-go?

"You really don't need to have this argument, because I'm going with you anyway," I interjected. "I'm not going to let you sideline me, when this is very much about my life, too. And neither of you will ever concede to the other, so you don't have much of a choice."

SEVEN

THE SHADE

Kathryn shook in his arms after the—for her—unusual sensation of teleportation. The startled look on her face reminded him of his own first experience with that part of his magic, and how he'd quivered like a leaf, too, much to the amusement of his teacher—the same man they were here to visit now.

The Shade indulged his urge to pull her closer to soothe her with his presence. A surge of male pride rushed through his blood when she gratefully pressed herself against his body for a few, blissful moments in an effort to stem her shaking. His cock instantly rose to the occasion, pressing eagerly against her stomach and straining against the fabric of his suit in its effort to reach her tantalizing warmth. He smiled wryly, continually amused by how his body acted like a desperate teenager around his woman.

Kathryn noticed it too. She jerked when she felt the firm press against her abdomen and pulled back, separating the contact, before shooting him and admonishing glare.

As if he could help the constantly churning ache in his

poor balls. He grabbed her by the chin and pulled her in for a quick kiss, enjoying her sputtering surprise turning to soft compliance with a little whimper as much as he enjoyed the tingling warmth of her lips. Yeah, she was as affected by him as he was by her.

The air crackled in front of them, and above Kathryn's blonde hair he saw Lightning's familiar red-and-charcoal clad figure appear. The annoyance in his enemy's eyes turned to anger when he spotted them.

"What the fuck, Shade? You were the one who told *me* no teleporting yesterday, remember?"

The Shade flicked his tongue out to dart it over the seam of Kathryn's lips, silently promising her much more at the earliest convenience, before he slowly pulled back to level a contemptuous stare at Lightning. "I trust me, not you. And I didn't fancy her puking all over me if we were to do the full trip by running."

Lightning glared at him with murderous intent. The Shade tensed his muscles in anticipation of a possible attack, but it didn't happen. Instead, the other supe grabbed Kathryn by the shoulders and pulled her out of his loose grip and into his own. She made some protesting noises, probably at being manhandled, that neither of them paid any mind.

"Do that again, Shade, and you'll regret it."

The Shade growled low in his throat and rolled his shoulders in a display of his bulging muscles. What was it about that girl that had all his most primitive instincts come rushing to the surface? At least Lightning was too deep in his own impulses to ridicule him. He bared his teeth and tugged Kathryn closer to his chest, ignoring her attempt at resistance. When he bent his head and claimed her mouth in a possessive kiss, she stopped pushing against him and seemed to melt under his touch as easily as she had under The Shade's lips.

The lack of anger in his chest at the scene surprised The Shade somewhat. Just the thought of Lightning taking her from him made rage pound in his temples, and when he'd first seen his full claim on the back of her neck, all he could think about was restating his own right to her... But seeing his enemy touch her intimately? Didn't seem to ruffle his otherwise volatile emotions when it came to her in the slightest. In fact, his cock twitched eagerly in his pants as he looked at Lightning's mouth move slowly against Kathryn's, while his hands caressed her full, voluptuous ass in a highly suggestive manner.

Had to be the damn, wonky magic in the claiming mark. Maybe their powers had mixed on her neck somehow, and they were now tied together through her?

That disturbing thought quelled his erection somewhat, and he shook his head to clear it of the cold dread that threatened to settle. "If you're done marking your territory like a common dog, maybe we can get going? Mirome has undoubtedly been made aware of our presence by now." He nodded toward a camera that was pointed at them.

Lightning ignored him while he pressed a few more teasing kisses to Kathryn's lips as his hands traveled up underneath her shirt. She jerked and squirmed against him, finally pulling her head back.

"Stop that! God, you two and your pheromones! Could we please focus on this meeting now?"

He couldn't stop the sly grin from spreading on his lips at the small woman's obvious frustration with her own reaction to their pheromones. There was a certain pleasure in making her body surrender despite her brain's obvious reluctance, and it seemed Lightning shared his sentiment, because when their eyes met for a short moment, he was wearing the same, smug expression as The Shade.

"Sure thing, Kittykat." Lightning didn't budge for her attempts at shoving him away, opting to wrap a possessive arm over her shoulders so he could easily guide her through the narrow alleyway that led to the rundown building where Mirome's more well-known lair was hidden. After a few moments, she gave up her resistance and let him lead her, though she was obviously sulking.

The Shade didn't bother disrupting the other man's clear marking of his territory—he'd felt the same urge when Lightning teleported with her the day before and there had been that short, terrifying moment where he'd thought he'd never see her again. As much as he despised the hero, he couldn't fault him for needing to reassure himself—and her—of his continued claim.

He followed them to the heavy metal door marking the only entry point for visitors, and hung back when Lightning rapped a knuckle against it. He trusted Mirome, as the only exception when it came to other supes, but it had been a long while since he'd been around his lair. There was no telling who might be watching.

The door ripped open with a bang seconds later, making Kathryn jump from shock and reel back. Lightning stopped her easily by tightening his arm as he leveled a broad smile at the man in the door.

"Mirome, old friend. Answering the door like a commoner now?"

"How could I not, once I saw my two boys arrive? Together, no less!" The brightly clad supe stepped aside with a flourish of his long sleeve, gesturing for them to enter. Lightning led Kathryn, who seemed to be doing her best not to stare at the flamboyant man with her mouth open, in, and The Shade followed, his muscles relaxing somewhat. If Mirome opened his own door, there was nothing threatening his compound. If there was one place he'd always felt safe, apart from his own hidden base, it was in the company of the superhuman who had trained him as a young man.

"And you brought the human girl, who has everyone aflutter with gossip?" Inside the dark corridor, Mirome turned around to level a curious stare at Kathryn. "I take it your dual claim is why you're here?"

The Shade grimaced. "Not exactly. We need to talk about Bright. We can't let his transgression against our human go unpunished, or the entire community will think she's an easy target to get to either of us."

"We were hoping you knew something about him that we don't," Lightning added. "Specifically, anything about his relations with the mayor."

Mirome's curious smile dropped as if someone had flipped a switch, his gaze darkening. "I was afraid you might want revenge. In the eyes of the community, he was in his right to detain her. You both best forget about him, and make sure the girl is kept somewhere safe. Trust me, nothing good will come from pursuing this."

"You know we can't do that," Lightning said. "If we don't take care of him, it will be the end of us. Will you help us?"

Their old teacher sighed. "If you insist, I will at the very least hear you out. Come, bring the girl to the basement so we can talk."

"Excuse me, *basement*?" Kathryn's indignant tone made The Shade cringe and glance at Mirome, who looked downright stunned that a human would speak to him in such a tone.

"I'm not going to any *basement*—I'm staying right here, with Lightning and The Shade, thank you very much."

Where he should have felt annoyance at her lip, or perhaps even embarrassment that his human outright confronted his old teacher—the one man that had ever held any sort of authority over him, from the sheer respect he'd commanded—The Shade instead fought back a smile. As soft and vulnerable as her humanity made her, and as traumatized as she'd obviously been by her run-in with Bright, she clearly still had plenty of spine left. He'd liked that about her from the night he'd shadowed her into the dark and dangerous industrial quarter in her search for answers, and he was pleased that her brush with superhuman society hadn't strangled that part of her.

Judging from Mirome's shocked expression, he certainly wasn't used to being denied by a human. He quickly recovered, though, and turned a disapproving stare framed by his trademark pearl-and-feathers mask at first The Shade and then Lightning.

"That girl needs discipline."

The Shade quelled the immediate image of Kathryn chained to his wide, four-poster bed that statement conjured. He glanced at her, and saw outrage plastered across her cute, round face. Yeah, compared to other, claimed humans, she was undoubtedly spoiled, but he liked her that way—free-willed and kinda obnoxious. No other woman he'd met while dressed as The Shade had had the guts to stand up to him like she did.

"She is not a slave, Mirome." Lightning's voice was unusually clipped, and it dawned on The Shade that—unlike him—Lightning had taken up a protective stance, carefully wedging his shoulder in between Kathryn and the man criticizing her. To The Shade's dismay, he realized that his enemy was protecting her, when he himself had failed to react. It didn't matter that Mirome was no threat to her—he had stood passive and let Lightning assume the position as her primary protector. The instincts tied to the mark he'd given her and anchored somewhere behind his ribs flared, squashing any rational thoughts on the matter.

His hand landed on her shoulder before he realized he'd even moved, his lips pulling up in a silent snarl of warning at their host.

Fuck, why couldn't he think straight when it came to her? He didn't fight the pull from his magic core, like Lightning obviously did, but it was still a novel—and not entirely pleasant—sensation of not being fully in control of himself.

Mirome gave him a contemptuous stare, and The Shade had enough decency to smother his aggressive facial expression. "I see. Regardless, what you wish to discuss is not suitable for human ears. If you want my help, she goes to the human quarters in the basement for the duration of your visit."

It was a reasonable request—Mirome was not used to treating claimed humans as more than servants, at best, and it was technically against their rules to allow a human as much knowledge of their ways as he and Lightning already had revealed to Kathryn. But... just the thought of not having her in his line of sight made his stomach turn. Those hellish hours where she'd been in Bright's hands had killed any and all desire to let her walk around unsupervised. A glance at Lightning's pinched lips told him that the other supe was as reluctant to follow their old teacher's command.

"Oh, whatever." Kathryn folded her arms across her chest with a huff and glared at Mirome in what could only be described as a highly insulting manner. "If you need to treat people like lesser beings to feel better about yourself, just because we don't all fly around shooting lasers out of our eyeballs, then fine. I'll go sit in Human Daycare and wait for Your Mightiness to impart your knowledge to worthier creatures."

The Shade did his best to conceal his snort of laughter behind a cough, somehow managing to send his human a chiding look. She only glared in return. It would seem she'd lost her inherent fear of him somewhere along the line.

"I'll take her," Lightning said, breaking the awkward silence following Kathryn's less than subtle display of dissatisfaction. "C'mon, Kittykat. Maybe someone will feed you so that blood sugar doesn't drop any lower, huh?"

Kathryn's reply was drowned out by the rush of anger in The Shade's veins when his enemy pulled her away from his light grasp on her shoulder, and began leading her deeper into Mirome's lair. It would be a cold day in hell before he let Lightning go anywhere alone with her again.

Instead of roaring out the challenge building in his throat, he reined in his embarrassing instincts that had his entire body throbbing to punch Lightning for pulling her out of his grasp, and followed the two. As surely as if he'd been leashed to the little human currently bitching about elitism and racism to no one in particular.

He could sense Mirome trailing behind them, and knew the older man would undoubtedly have more than one comment about their arrangement, once they were in private quarters. He grimaced, wishing he knew what there was to say about it. Truth was, he had no idea why he didn't feel like ripping Lightning's throat out for thinking he had any sort of claim to Kathryn—only when he thought his enemy might take her away from him did his instincts flare.

Not that that mattered in the long run. Once Bright was dealt with and Kathryn was safe, he'd kill off the hero and then explore exactly what it was that made this woman so different from all the others. Primarily with his cock.

"We'll come get you as soon as we're done. You'll be safe here." Lightning had stopped in front of the only wooden door in the narrow brick hallway. He touched Kathryn's cheek in an apologetic gesture and leaned over to open the door.

"Feel free to ask my humans for food," Mirome supplied from behind The Shade. "Tell them you're my most honored guests' human and they won't hesitate to obey."

It seemed like a peace offering, and Kathryn's angry glare broke for a moment, the corners of her mouth slipping up into a grateful smile as she stepped through the door, but before she managed to thank their host, Mirome turned to him and Lightning. "As for you two, I'm sure you're eager to be introduced to my newest crop of pleasure girls before we get down to business."

EIGHT

LIGHTNING

The shocked expression flashing across Kathryn's features at Mirome's casual remark was the last thing either of them saw as the door was slammed in her face.

Lightning gave their host a measured look. As wise as their old teacher may be, he had never been above pettiness, and Lightning was fairly certain he had purposely tried to hurt the human bold enough to give him attitude. Judging from the look on her face, it had worked.

As much as that place behind the ribs where the magic connecting him to Kathryn seemed to be rooted throbbed to soothe his temperamental little human, he couldn't deny a certain level of satisfaction in knowing that the thought of them with other women did, in fact, hurt her. He hadn't managed to figure out exactly what his possessive urge to hover around her 24/7 meant, but the volatile instincts awakened with his marking of her definitely appreciated that she didn't want him to sleep with someone else.

Unless, of course, her jealousy was reserved for The Shade.

Lightning gave his enemy a resentful side-glance as the three of them walked down the corridor toward Mirome's private chambers. Why the city's most feared villain wasn't terrified of the obvious pull to the girl was beyond him, but it was irritating as all hell. Bad enough that he was obviously competing for her affections with his archenemy—the chance that he was losing was real.

No one spoke until the door to Mirome's lavish office closed behind them with a smooth click. Their host turned around by his desk, fingers pressed against each other and a small smile gracing his lips.

"So. Shall I call on a couple of girls? The tension rolling off you two suggests it's most certainly needed."

"No." Lightning frowned at The Shade, irritated with his echoed denial. If he'd opted to fuck another woman, Lightning had a sneaking suspicion his favor with Kathryn would have dropped drastically. But no. The one time in his life the goon opted to do the right thing obviously had to be when his normally moral free approach would have been most welcome.

Perhaps The Shade was also plagued with a complete disinterest in any female anatomy not occupying Kathryn's deliciously rounded body.

Fucking mark.

"How very interesting." Mirome's eyes sparkled ominously behind his extravagant mask. "And I suppose this sudden lack of need to fuck anything that moves is related to your recent and rather embarrassing public claim on the fat little spitfire sulking in my basement at the moment?"

"Don't even think about insulting her." The hissed words came from The Shade, but the low, threatening growl resonating in the office originated from Lightning's own chest.

"My, my. So fiercely protective. Does she know how lucky she is? I bet she doesn't. I bet you two don't even understand what's going on."

Lightning clenched his fists and swallowed the angry sound. "We're not here to discuss her, Mirome. We need to know what you can tell us about Bright."

Mirome's face lit up in a playful smile. "You don't! Ha, I bet that must be driving you both mad. Tell me, are you not the least bit curious as to why a simple human has instincts you never knew about flaring like a bonfire? Or am I wrong? Do you not have a messy, sticky web of icky *feelings* for the girl?"

Lightning exchanged an uncomfortable glance with The Shade. As much as he didn't want to think too hard about his own reaction to that blasted mark, he did want to know what the fuck was going on.

"Tell us—" The Shade began. Though his voice was gruff, it didn't erase the pleading note to it. "What do you know about our connection with her, teacher?"

"Ah." Mirome tilted his head and gave them a sly look. "I suppose it depends. When you first saw her, what made you choose to mark her?"

"She needed protection," Lightning muttered, leveling a glare at The Shade. "*He* marked her in a childish attempt at pissing me off."

The older man rolled his eyes. "I don't care about the excuses you gave yourself. I mean the real reason. You aren't noble enough to claim a human just for her own protection, or you would have had several hundreds by now. And you," he pointed a teal-tipped nail at The Shade, "wouldn't take your first human servant just to annoy him. So tell me—what was it that made you decide that this girl was worth your mark?"

Lightning stared at The Shade, willing him to speak first. But he didn't, the fucker—he just raised an eyebrow at Lightning at his stare and crossed his arms. Stubborn as a mule.

"I had to," Lightning finally said. "I saw her, and I knew she had to be mine. I don't know why, only that my magic wanted—no, *needed* me to."

The Shade nodded his consent, choosing to stay quiet. Coward.

"Ha, that's what I thought!" Mirome swiveled around in a colorful flurry of silken robes before perching elegantly on his desk, legs crossed and hand wrapped around a knee. He watched them with cat-like amusement glowing behind the blue eyes marking their race. "You, my dear boys, have found a mate."

"A what now?"

"A mate." Mirome unclasped his hands from his knee and waved it dramatically. "It seems to be cyclical, this flare in our magic to spread its spark. It's happened since the very beginning. As you well know, we are the result of our noble ancestors breeding with humans, too. Once every few centuries, the magic craves new blood, and so it makes *you* crave the one human on this planet who will be a receptive vessel to your unique essence. If we were a more sentimental race, maybe we would call it *the soulmate principle*. In reality, it's just a convenient way for our ancestors' superior genes to spread to a slightly wider pool. She is breeding stock, your mouthy human."

The Shade frowned. "But the magic never transfers when we have children with humans? Everyone knows this."

Lightning gave him an incredulous stare. Really? *That* was his most pressing question right now?

"Ah, everyone knows that you cannot breed the magic into a regular human, true. Very few know that, for some of us, there is exactly one human who will let your power take root. It's amusing, of course, that you two share one. I don't think that's happened before, but who knows. I doubt anyone would have been keen to share such information. Can you imagine? Double dipping your wife with a brother. You'd never even know if the children were really yours or his."

Whoa, *wife? Children?* The room seemed to spin, slowly picking up speed, and sweat formed on Lightning's forehead underneath the mask. He forced his mind away from those two terrifying words, focusing instead on something he could analyze without risking a goddamn panic attack.

"Why is this not something every supe learns about as he grows up? Why have we never heard of a single supe-human couple? And how do you know about this, when even Bright and the Council seemed oblivious to what could be causing... this?"

Mirome's smile quirked up at the corner. "Would you have made the strength of your attachment to this human known if you'd had a choice? If this was widely known, the less savory of us would be hunting for mated couples. These deliciously breakable little humans make for such good blackmail material, as long as their owner cares enough about them. Did you never wonder why our most sacred rule is to never go after someone's marked human? Who cares if the little thing you picked up for their superb blowjob skills gets killed? But a *mate...?* Widespread ignorance is the best defense. And how I know?" He winked. "Who better to be our race's Secret Keeper than the man who killed the last? It's in the job description. Whoever kills the previous one gets to pick up the mantle. Of course, I had no idea that when I offed Lithica, she would hand over all these delicious secrets. I consider it a perk. I did always enjoy a good, juicy secret—like the one you two now share."

Lightning scrubbed both hands over his face. He did vaguely remember Lithica's death. She had been one of the old and great ones, and he'd had no idea Mirome was responsible for her murder. Not that it mattered now—there were more pressing concerns to deal with.

"Kathryn will give us a Dragonborn child."

Such as that.

Lightning winced as The Shade's quiet statement forced his mind back to the one thing he didn't know how to cope with. One look at The Shade, however, and it was obvious that the villain was horrifyingly okay with the idea. His eyes shone with an odd reverence, and his jaw was set with determination. As far as Lightning could tell, he was ready to go knock up their unsuspecting woman right this moment. Who knew The Shade had fostered dreams of procreating? Or perhaps it was a new revelation, and he was just basking in dreams of taking over the world with an army of evil little offspring. Lightning gave him an acrid look.

"She won't give us anything if we don't figure out how to get rid of Bright. Can we please focus on what we came here for? Or would you rather plan car pools and packed lunches while *I* eliminate the threat to her life?"

The last part earned him a dark look, but it did at least seem to pull the criminal out of his disturbing procreation plans.

"He's right. We need to kill Bright before we uncover

more of this, Mirome. Will you help us? Will you help us protect the future of our race?"

He did always have a flair for the dramatic, even back when they were young men training together. But then again, so did their teacher, so it was probably a decent tactic. Lightning smothered his eye roll and looked to Mirome, setting his mouth in a serious line. "We need your help, old teacher."

The older man's smile was no longer present, his eyes dark with unease, but as he glanced from The Shade to Lightning, he sighed, his shoulders slumping. "You don't know what you're asking, Bright... he is stronger than you think. And sly. He's got allies where you least expect them. Don't fight him—join his ranks, or flee the city with your mate. If you don't, you will die."

NINE

So what if they were having sex with two gorgeous, slender, long-legged women? Who cared, anyway? It wasn't like I was their *girlfriend*, or something ridiculously human like that.

I stabbed a gravy-covered piece of potato, picturing Mirome's smirking face as my fork pierced the tuber. Whatever my messed up relationship with the two superhumans was, no one had ever promised any sort of fidelity. Heck, I was sleeping with both of them, so it wasn't like I had much of a moral high ground to stand on.

It didn't make the twisting jealousy in my gut any easier to handle, though.

"Is it true that you belong to both The Shade *and* Lightning?"

I glanced up from my plate to the man leaning on the kitchen counter, eyes eagerly locked on my sulking form. I knew that look well—it was approximately what I looked like as well, when I was fishing for particularly juicy gossip.

"Yeah," I said, carefully putting my fork down on the

plate as I examined his older but very handsome face and slender physique. He had probably been in the household for some time now, taken in in his younger days for his good looks. And he probably knew all the gossip that Mirome did, judging from his approach now. I'd been left on my own after a sulky young woman had slapped a stew up on a plate for me when I said who I was and asked for food, but this guy didn't stay away like the other humans that had left the room with my arrival.

I might have been relegated to the kids table, but maybe I could still get something useful out of this visit. I mean, apart from knowing that the two men I felt way more for than what any sane woman should were busy having sex with someone who wasn't me.

"How did that happen?" my new friend asked. He crossed the floor and slid down on the bench by the table right across from me, eyes eagerly scanning my face as if the explanation as to why not one but *two* superhumans had chosen to claim me could be found somewhere behind my obvious plainness. "Their hatred of each other is infamous."

I sighed dramatically. "Lightning was trying to keep me safe—some really bad people were after me, and in the end, he could only save my life by marking me. But he didn't want to force himself on me, so he didn't complete the claim that night. He said he wanted to give me the choice. Then, The Shade found me in an alley one night." I lowered my voice to add tension to the story. I'd never been the greatest story-teller, but Mirome's servant seemed enthralled. He leaned across the table, lips slightly parted with complete focus.

"Lightning had to go out that night, and I... I was foolish and thought I'd look into the bad people myself. But they found me first, and nearly... nearly killed me." The emotion in my voice was genuine this time. The memory of that night in the alley where I thought I was going to get raped and murdered still brought a lump to my throat and caused chills to creep down my spine. "The Shade saw my mark and decided to save me, to use me against Lightning somehow. But he... he changed his mind. And decided I had to be his." It wasn't a completely truthful explanation of the events that had led me down this path, but it held enough truth to resonate with the gossip-hungry servant.

"I bet Lightning was unhappy," he breathed.

I grimaced, thinking back to Lightning's flip-out in the mayor's office when he'd discovered The Shade's mark on my nape. "Yeah. He was pretty angry. But then he decided to claim me fully. Because he'd already put a preliminary mark on me, he was able to go through The Shade's mark. And now I belong to both of them."

"That's... you're very lucky," he said, and to my surprise, envy flickered in his brown eyes.

I wasn't sure I would use the term *lucky* to describe my current predicament, but I nodded nonetheless. Presumably, most humans who got marked by a supe would feel honored, given how the general public viewed them.

"They don't even have any other humans, do they?" my dining companion asked. "No one's ever mentioned anything, and we hear most of what goes on in the supe world here."

It was nice to get my suspicions about the level of intel available in Mirome's human quarters confirmed. I shook my head and took a few sips from the wineglass next to my mostly empty plate. "No, it's just me."

"The sex must be amazing."

I coughed, taken by surprise by his brazen statement enough to choke on my wine.

"I share Mirome with almost twenty other claimed humans, and he's still almost too much for me to handle. Of course, it was different when I was a young man—but still. Being the only human to take on *two* supes' needs... you must go through an awful lot of lube."

Blood heated my cheeks, undoubtedly coloring them as red as two shiny tomatoes. Maybe it was the norm for claimed humans to freely talk about private stuff like this. I cleared my throat and determinately avoided his curious gaze. "Ah, yeah... Um, so anyway... how long have you been with Mirome?"

"Twenty years." He smiled, pride reflecting in his eyes. "I was his third."

"Where're the two first?" The question just slipped out, and judging from the frown on the servant's lips, it wasn't appreciated. He still answered me, though, seemingly not willing to lose his newest source of gossip despite my accidental rudeness.

"They got replaced. As did the fourth, fifth, sixth, seventh, eighth, ninth... you get the picture. He likes me the best, hence why I'm still here."

"You must be very important to him," I agreed, hoping my attempt at placating him wasn't too obvious. He was my best shot at trying to pump whatever information I could out of this so far pretty disastrous visit. "I can only hope my supes will treasure me as much in a few years."

Even though I told myself I was just playing into this guy's supe-obsession, it still hurt to force the last part out. I didn't exactly want to be anyone's treasured pet, hoping that my services were appreciated enough to not get dumped like yesterday's trash, nor did I feel all that warm and fuzzy about my connection to either man. The thought of them both with some woman's legs wrapped around their hips made me want to gag, and anger fueled by hurt burned like acid in my veins.

The servant sniffed, still eying me with a measure of hesitance. And pride. "Yes, I am. He trusts me and treats me almost like an equal."

I nodded, not bothering to ask why, if he was treated almost as Mirome's equal, he was hanging out in the basement with the rest of us unworthy humans. This man had built his entire life around the superhuman who'd claimed him in his youth. Pointing out how, even though he may well be the favorite, he was still nothing more than a toy or a pet to his beloved master, would be cruel. I looked at his proud face with the fine lines he had tried to cover with makeup, and felt pity. Had he even had a choice, back when he was first claimed? Had he had an inkling that he wouldn't be in charge of his own life ever again?

A cold tremor made its way down my spine. Was this the future that was in store for me, too? I couldn't deny that I felt myself drawn to both the two mysterious and dangerous men who had come into my life to claim possession over me, however much the rational side of me protested. How long would it be before my unhealthy crush developed into something a lot darker—something that would suck me in and never let me go again?

And if I ever found that answer... would it even matter? Was I doomed from the moment I laid eyes on Lightning in that coffee shop?

"He always leaves me in charge of the household when

we have important guests," my table buddy continued, drawing me out of my morose thoughts with a self-important sniff. "I certainly don't know of any other marked humans who would have been allowed to speak in their supe's presence during a visit from the mayor."

TEN

"Wait, the *mayor* visited Mirome?" I just about managed not to gape at the man in front of me, in a last ditch-effort not to tip him off that he'd just handed out more than a bit of juicy gossip. My surprised gasp seemed to have done the trick, though, because the servant clamped up like an oyster, giving me a suspicious stare.

"I am not at liberty to discuss my master's guest list," he said, managing to get more than a whiff of snootiness in there, despite the fact that he'd volunteered information about said *guest list* mere moments ago. "And if I may offer you some advice—if you are caught asking intrusive questions like this, your supes are going to get rid of you sooner rather than later."

This time, my mouth did drop open, though more from the nerve of him rather than surprise.

Luckily for both of us, the door to the kitchen opened just then, revealing Lightning's bulky mass. Behind him, I could just catch a glimpse of The Shade's midnight-black suit.

"Kathryn, we're ready."

Despite the revelation that the mayor had visited The Shade's and Lightning's trusted friend's house, the comment still reminded me of being picked up from daycare—which reignited my previous, gloomy thoughts about the girls they'd been offered and my future with the two.

I gave Lightning a sullen look, but got up from the table nonetheless. Arguing with them now, or trying to bring up "The Talk," while we were still at Mirome's house would not be a smart choice. Even if I did have an irrational—and nearly insurmountable—desire to slap both of them. Hard.

Lightning's gloved hand closed around mine when I reached the door, encompassing it fully. He pulled me close to him the moment we were out in the dark hallway, letting me feel all his torso's strong muscles through the suit fabric, he was holding me that tight.

Another large hand closed around my shoulder, and I didn't have to look behind me to know that it belonged to The Shade. It was odd, really—though jealousy was still tearing at me like a rabid dog, something about they way they touched me seemed so possessive, like maybe they had been as unhappy about our short separation as I was.

Mirome was nowhere to be seen, and I assumed he had said his goodbyes to the two supes already and—clearly— didn't see the need to see me off. I was just a human, after all.

I frowned as I looked back at my dinner companion. I hadn't asked his name, and he hadn't offered it. As our eyes met, I knew it was because neither of us found it important. He was Mirome's servant, the third human he had ever claimed. And that was all he was.

I couldn't help the wave of sadness for him as Lightning and The Shade led me through the hallway and out into the deserted alley that hid the entrance to their old teacher's house, but there was nothing I could do to help him. And he would never let me, even if there was. He felt blessed for his lot in life, and as I felt myself press against my two escorts without conscious thought to my actions, I knew why. Once you had let one of their kind into your heart, you were lost forever. And I had opened myself up to two.

<hr>

"SO WHAT DID he tell you? Or are you not allowed to discuss that with a mere mortal slave?" The moment my stomach stopped heaving after the teleport back, I wrenched my shoulder and arm out of both supes' grip and crossed the room to lean against my couch, arms folded.

Lightning didn't quite manage to hide his eye roll at my standoffish demeanor, but instead of coming with some sort of smart remark—as per his usual style—he only sighed.

"You're not a slave, kitten," The Shade said, his tone calm and rational, as if explaining himself to an unreasonable child mid-tantrum. "Have either of us made you do something you didn't want to?"

I considered mentioning the first time he had sex with me in the alley, but as much as I wished I could deny it, I'd wanted him. Wholeheartedly.

"I didn't exactly want to be claimed like a commodity by two shady superhumans with rampant hormones and serious personality issues," I snapped instead.

This time, Lightning didn't bother to try and hide his eyeroll. "You're welcome for saving your ass—repeatedly. Now, are you going to tell us what has you so goddamn bitchy all of a sudden, or are we just going to have to guess?"

I fought back an embarrassed blush at his comment. Yeah, I was probably being pretty bitchy right now, but I couldn't suppress the feelings of betrayal and burning jealousy when the two men that had my emotions all messed up and confused had left me behind to go sleep with someone else. But I didn't want to admit to that. I didn't want to admit that I had feelings for either man, that could lead to jealousy.

"I'm not bitchy—I'm just really annoyed at being left in the basement like a disobedient dog. This is my life too, and I don't appreciate being kept out of the loop. So tell me—what did this old teacher of yours have to say?"

The two supes glanced at each other, and I frowned at the uncomfortable look that passed between them. Something had obviously happened during their meeting with Mirome. "What?"

"Nothing all that useful," Lightning said, giving one last lingering look to his enemy before finally catching my gaze with his glowing blue eyes. "At least, not what we were hoping for. He more than hinted that Bright's reach extends so far and deep that we won't be able to beat him."

I frowned. "I thought you said Mirome would be able to help for sure?"

"Yes. That he's under the impression that there's no way to beat Bright is... concerning," The Shade said. "He is old, and sly. If *he* believes Bright so strong he's unbeatable, then we need to give serious consideration to just leaving the city. Go somewhere where you will be safe."

Wait, what? "Whoa, hold on!" I stared from The Shade to Lightning, refusing to believe what I'd just heard. "You can't be serious—you are actually thinking about letting him *win*?"

The Shade grimaced. "It's not ideal."

"You're damn right it's not!" I was still so shocked that they would even consider leaving St. Anthony behind that I didn't even pause to consider that I was the reason. "What about all the innocent people who're going to get caught up in this? Who knows how many humans will end up dead because of this? Not to mention, I don't think trusting the word of a man who's inviting the mayor over for dinner is such a wise idea."

There was a moment's pause as both men stared at me.

"What did you say?"

I arched an eyebrow at them, feeling just a tiny bit smug for having uncovered something that they seemingly hadn't known about. "I take it Mirome didn't share that little tidbit up at the adult's table? I talked to one of his claimed humans —his favorite. He said the mayor had been by. I know you've got history with the guy, but maybe he isn't as trustworthy as you thought, if he's hanging out with the mayor. We know Wilkins is involved with Bright somehow, so who knows how Mirome fits into it all." I finally stopped talking when I realized the sudden tension in the air. It made the hairs on my arms stand on end, as if an electric current was brushing against my skin. "What?"

"Taking servant gossip for the absolute truth isn't wise, Kathryn." The Shade's lips were pinched into a narrow line, and I was pretty sure he was scowling behind the mask. "Our relationship with Mirome goes back a very long time. He was our teacher, back in the day. He's not one for siding with scum like Bright, and he would never work against us on something this serious."

"I get that, but you can't just ignore a lead like this. Why would a superhuman like your teacher invite the mayor over? I'm telling you, something's going on, and we should look into it—or at the very least not be ready to drop everything and flee the city just because your friend says so, when he might be involved—"

"Either that servant lied, or there is a reasonable explanation," Lightning interrupted. "Mirome was more than a teacher. He was our mentor for years, Kathryn. We know him better than you do some gossipy servant. I know you want to help solve what's going on with Bright and the mayor, but you have to trust us that we know best what goes on in the supe community. And what doesn't."

It was too much. I felt my arms starting to tremble, as if they were somehow detached from my body. Angrily, I clenched my fists until my nails bit into my palms. "Oh, really? So I guess what you're saying is that you really do agree with him, as well? That us humans belong in the basement and aren't worthy of your superior intellect? That I have no clue how to find out any valuable information, even though I was the one who uncovered the connection between the mayor and Bright's weapon? If you're so goddamn blinded by your worship of this one man, I guess I'll just go sit down and be quiet, while you two fuck his mind controlled sex slaves and find out absolutely nothing of value!"

As soon as the last part slipped past my lips, I wished I could have taken it back. I didn't want to expose the nagging jealousy seething in my gut to them, because I didn't want them to know how vulnerable I truly was. Being marked by two superhumans was bad enough—letting them know that I... *felt* something for them? That had disaster written all over it.

"Is that what this is all about?" Though Lightning's voice was carefully neutral, I couldn't help but notice the satisfied glint in his eyes. "You're angry with him for offering us other women?"

The heat in my face spoke of a most impressive blush. Irritated, I folded my arms across my chest. "I don't care who or what you fuck. I just don't like hanging around waiting for y'all to be done. '*This*' is about getting to the bottom of the mess you two dragged me into."

"You don't care one teeny, tiny bit?" The Shade didn't bother hiding the teasing tone from his voice. "Because you looked like you cared an awful lot when Mirome suggested we enjoy his girls."

I'm not sure what was strongest—the hurt, or the anger welling up like a tsunami from deep within. Bad enough that they'd done it, but mocking me with it?

"Fuck you, both of you!" I hissed and turned around, prepared to storm out of the apartment though I had no clue where I could possibly go that wouldn't end up with me captured again. My pulse pounded in my temples, and I knew that if I didn't get out of there, the lump in my throat would come up as big, ugly sobs of hurt and humiliation.

Two large hands, one on each of my arms, stopped me before I'd taken more than a step.

"There's no need to get in a huff. You are the only woman I'm interested in fucking, Kittykat."

"Likewise," The Shade purred. "And all this talk about *fucking* is starting to get to me. It's been days since I've felt your soft body clench around me."

I swallowed thickly at the sudden change in conversation and tension in the room. Where it had been unpleasant and prickly before, the air was now thick with insinuation—and undoubtedly their blasted pheromones. I closed my eyes to steel myself and blink back the few tears that had managed to escape.

The hand on my right arm slipped down to my waist and up under my shirt, stroking across my soft flesh.

"Want me to show you just how special you are, baby?" Lightning's voice had taken on a seductive purr to rival The Shade's. His fingertips dances across my stomach, teasing my skin into goosebumps. "How there's no one but you? Would that make you feel better?"

The traitorous tingle down my spine rooted itself between my thighs. I blushed again, ashamed of my body's easy response. No wonder I had no control of the situation when I couldn't even stop myself from pining like a lovesick cat in heat just from a few sweet words and heated touches. Frustrated, I shook off their hands and stepped away. "I don't need to be made to '*feel better.*' I need to be respected like a person with a mind of their own, and you both seem incapable of that."

Hands grasped my waist none too gently and pulled me back with a sudden jerk, flattening my back against Lightning's strong torso.

"Oh, I'll respect you every step of the way. But you need this, and so do I." His voice was hoarse and spoke to that tingling sensation low down in my abdomen as his breath brushed against my ear. When he bit the back of my neck, I couldn't hold back a groan, nor the instant trickle of moisture from deep inside. "Why would I want another woman when all I can think about is you? You really believe I would have come for you, with him, if anyone else could satisfy the craving I have?"

I wish I could have said that I stepped away from his grasp again, but as much as what was left of my cognitive function wanted me to, the heat from him seemed to melt my muscles and turn my body into complacent pudding. The words he spoke, the way his hands felt against my skin as they traveled up underneath my top to cup my breasts over the cotton bra... My brain fogged over, allowing my weak body to press back against the hero, melting into his embrace. He was right. After everything I'd been through, I needed this—needed the reassurance of his desire and the release from the tumultuous emotions of fear, anger and jealousy that seemed to have taken up permanent residence in my body these past few days.

Lightning's low growl of satisfaction was echoed from The Shade's chest. I cracked my eyelids open in time to see the dark clad man close the two steps that separated us, his eyes aflame with need and possessiveness. He wrapped both gloved hands around my face and tilted it up, capturing my lips with his a second later.

His kiss was scorching. I moaned softly into his mouth as my senses were overwhelmed with his presence, parting my lips for his demanding tongue without resistance. Teasing fingers pinched my nipples, making me moan again and a stronger current of desire travel down to the tense nub of nerves between my thighs.

If I'd still had the ability to process more than just sensations, maybe I would have startled at the realization that I was sandwiched between the two most infamous superhumans in the city, feeling The Shade's growing erection press against my stomach from the front, and Lightning's against my back. Perhaps the knowledge of what was happening— what I was allowing to happen—would have registered as disbelief or shame. But I wasn't. And it didn't.

By the time The Shade lifted his head to let me breathe,

my mind was spinning and my breathing was erratic. He slid his arms around me, clutching me tighter against his body by grabbing my ass in both hands, squeezing firmly at the ample flesh. I choked on a gasp when my burning clit rubbed against his rock hard erection, and then cried out when a sharp bite to the back of my neck and a firm pinch of my nipples made me jerk back as much as the hands on my ass would let me. Lightning wasn't happy with losing the closeness of my body.

The hero's hands slid from my breasts to my hips, trying to force me back again, but The Shade didn't budge. Instead, both men strengthened their grasp on me, fingers digging deep into my helpless flesh as both growled in warning at the other.

"*Ow!*" My yelp of pain stopped both their growling and their tug of war abruptly, but neither released their hold on my poor hips and ass. It also cleared my head of the fog of lust just a little.

"Look, maybe we should stop." My voice was breathless, and even I recognized how little conviction was in it. Perhaps that was why I got completely ignored.

I don't know what passed between the two men I was sandwiched between, but when I looked up I could see that The Shade was glaring at his enemy over my shoulder, rather than me. Then he nodded almost imperceptibly, and released his firm grip on my backside.

For a moment I thought they were indeed stopping, and a wave of disappointment swept over me. But before I could voice the protest forming on my lips, his hands swept to my side and grabbed my shirt, tugging it upward without pause.

Lightning let go of my hips and grabbed my arms, lifting them up so The Shade could pull my top off without pause.

My bra followed a second later, as did my pants and panties, and before I knew it, I was standing naked between them, my nipples tight from the sudden exposure to the cooler air.

"Oh!" I blinked, my startled outburst coming much too late. In front of me The Shade smirked and grabbed his own top, pulling it over his head in one fluid movement that let his newly revealed abs flex with mesmerizing strength.

His hands went to his pants next, but before I could revel in that glorious sight, Lightning spun me around to face him instead.

He too was suddenly topless, and I couldn't stop my eyes from roaming his ridiculously defined torso with hunger. I didn't get much of a chance to take in the sight, though, as Lightning lifted me up so I was forced to part my legs for his hips, and bent his head to my breasts, sucking a pert nipple into his mouth.

I groaned and clutched at the back of his head, my ankles crossing behind his back when my legs tried to clamp together around the sharp shocks of pleasure that shot from my nipple directly to my clit.

Lightning lashed his tongue at the small bud of flesh until it was almost painful with sensation, then moved to my other nipple. He sucked it hard enough for me to whimper with a delicious sort of pain, seemingly too lost in his own lust to be too refined with his attentions, but it didn't matter. My body yearned for the roughness, and I reveled in the strength of his desire, even as I mewled and writhed against his hold.

When he finally broke free and lifted his head back up to catch my gaze, his eyes were dark with raw and unbridled lust

"Are you wet for me, baby?" he said, the hoarseness of his voice making my pussy clench with longing.

I was pretty sure he could feel my dampness against his stomach, where my thighs were parted for his strong body, but I nodded nonetheless, biting down on my lower lip to stop a wanton moan from escaping.

"Yeah? All ready to take everything I've got for you?"

Before I could as much as nod my head in response this time, a frustrated growl sounded from behind me. "If you don't hurry the fuck up, I'll take care of her for you."

The truce between the two men was apparently pretty time-sensitive.

Lightning rolled his eyes before he brushed his lips over mine in a swift but gentle kiss that set my senses aflame with the wild and spicy flavor of him.

"I hope you are ready, because I'm going to fuck you good," he whispered in my ear. "Until you're so exhausted you won't think to let him continue."

Allow him to continue? I stared up into Lightning's glowing eyes, and it finally fully dawned on me what I was about to let happen. It wasn't just some kinky make-out session. No, I was going to have sex with the city's favored hero while his archenemy watched us... and then they'd swap.

If I'd been a moral sort of woman, the delayed realization of exactly the sort of depravities I was about to engage in should have made me deny them.

As it turned out, I wasn't anything close to a moral woman.

With a soft groan I arched my back, thrusting my breasts up toward the hero in invitation while grinding my already slickened nether lips against the hard stacks of his abdominal muscles. "Just take me. *Now!*"

The world *whooshed* around me, and then I was on my back on my bed, blinking up at Lightning's burning eyes. His lips pulled back in a silent snarl in a threat of the most carnal kind.

I raised up on my elbows to enjoy the view of his bare torso while he opened his pants, but was almost instantly pushed back down flat again. Lightning's strong hips pressed heavily between my thighs, anchoring me to the mattress as he climbed in over me.

"Sorry, princess," he rasped at my attempt to lift my hips up to grind my aching clit against his groin. "No foreplay today. I need you too much."

I frowned at the brazen comment and glanced at the terrifyingly thick cock in his hand. He wanted to put *that* inside of me with no warm up?

Lightning smirked, apparently following my train of thought from my stare. "Don't worry, you're ready." He dipped two fingers between us, dragging the tips through my folds in a slow taunt that made my hips rise again, before holding them up between us. They were soaked.

With a wink he drew both fingers in between his lips, moaning gutturally as he sucked them clean.

My pussy spasmed at the sight, the internal muscles fluttering as if they remembered the pleasure his mouth had caused me not all that long ago. I didn't get to dwell on the memories, though, because Lightning grabbed his hard length and drove it into me with no further pause.

"*Oh!*" The sensation of suddenly being *full* made my pussy clench down hard against the intrusion in an instinctive attempt to protect my innermost core. But it was too little too late, and the spasm only worked to increase the tension in my hypersensitive flesh, rubbing my g-spot deliciously against the brutal cock.

I cried out again and rocked my hips up to meet him as pleasure crashed through my nerve endings. As when we were together last, I was helpless to resist my own body's primal urges to submit and surrender to the strong, powerful man. His near-desperate thrusts that would have left me aching for days had I been any less wet and ready seemed to fill not only my clutching channel but also my mind, pounding his need for me into my very soul.

It was intoxicating. His energy lit every cell in my body aflame, and I knew that at that moment, I was the only thing, the only one, that could satisfy his deep, dark cravings. The truth I hadn't seen before blazed from his eyes as much as it did from his powerful hips—right then and there, he needed me more than life itself.

If I hadn't been gone on the pure rush of ecstasy coursing through my body from where he was pounding me mercilessly, the intensity of it all might have scared me. As it was, it only served to make a surge of fierce possessiveness rise in my body like wildfire.

"Mine! You're mine!" I gasped, before digging my nails into his shoulders in a frantic attempt to contain the molten pressure from his penetration that threatened to make me come undone. "Fuck, *harder!*"

Any girl with her wits still intact would never have asked a superhuman on the brink of losing control to fuck her harder. Sadly for me, I'd lost all grips on reality the moment he pushed inside of me all the way to my very core.

Lightning snarled and snapped his hips hard enough to make me yelp and my bed groan, but before I could gather my scattered thoughts enough to protest, he pressed the heel of one hand into my throbbing clit.

Everything turned white, and for one excruciating, drawn out moment, I was nothing but nerve endings and aching flesh—and my entire world was made up of the too-intense pleasure forced on me by my lover's hand against my helpless clit, underlined by the deep, ruthless thrusts that filled me so perfectly. Then, mercifully, I crested.

"Yes!" My entire body seized, making me convulse on the bed in spams that seemed to stem from my innermost core. I clung to Lightning's shoulders, whimpering and with my eyes squeezed shut while he brought me to completion.

When my orgasm finally started to ebb, he growled *"fuck!"* above me and stiffened. The hot rush of his semen flooded my channel in powerful jets less than a second later, his eyes screwed shut and his mouth twisted with soul deep pleasure.

I flopped down, exhausted and sated while he finished in me, rocking his hips gently for the last few moments of our lovemaking.

If you could call it lovemaking. My pussy pulsed somewhere behind the fog of afterglow, promising a less than comfortable day tomorrow. How was it that with these two, the roughest fuckings of my life felt like so much more than just primal sex?

Lightning finally opened his eyes and looked down with an expression in his blue gaze that made my heart flutter. His eyes roamed over my face, a questioning expression in them as if he wasn't quite sure what had just happened between us.

I smiled tiredly, too content on my endorphin high to be bothered by the hero's changeable moods, and lifted a lethargic hand up to touch the red lines I'd left without even realizing. "Sorry about that."

He looked at my hand on his shoulder, his mouth pursing in obvious puzzlement. Clearly, he hadn't noticed when it happened either.

I expected a smartass comeback of some sort, but when he looked at me again he only brushed his knuckles against my cheek in a tender caress. Then he pulled out, slowly enough to let my swollen channel get accustomed to the change. I still felt the loss all too keenly when he got off the bed and walked out of my field of vision with one last, lingering look at my sprawled-out form.

"Hey," I protested, rolling up on one arm to stop him from leaving so abruptly. But the glowing blue eyes I caught didn't belong to Lightning.

The Shade smirked and prowled closer, drawing my attention from Lightning. He had gotten fully naked at some point during my tryst with his enemy, save the ever-present black mask, and judging from the rock-hard erection jutting out in front of him, he had very much enjoyed the show.

Though my lower parts felt extremely well-used, a warm glow of anticipation flooded up from my abdomen at the sight of him. *Damn pheromones.*

"You may want to give me a moment." I made a vague gesture down my body to indicate the sticky fluids I could still feel dripping out of me without being too crass about it. "I need a short intermission."

The Shade scoffed and leapt agilely onto the bed so he could crawl in over my still-splayed form. "You can rest later, kitten. Right now, you need to get on your hands and knees and show me that sweet little cunt of yours."

I squawked in protest at his crude command, but truth

be told, it made my already molten body flush with primitive excitement.

"You can't seriously want to—*oh!*" I squealed belatedly when strong hands flipped me over with preternatural speed so I was suddenly face-down on the mattress, and grunted as The Shade pulled me back and up into position.

"Beautiful," he growled, letting thick fingers slide teasingly up through my soaked folds. "Soaked, open and ready to be taken and bred. Just like I need you."

Wait, what? *Bred?*

I didn't get a chance to ponder this particular strand of dirty talk as The Shade grabbed my hips in both hands, lined himself up against my sopping pussy and entered me in one long, smooth stroke.

"*Oh! God!*"

The Shade growled as he bottomed out, his fingers digging into my hips deep enough to bruise them. Not that I had the presence of mind to care. As before, my world narrowed in until all it contained was the hard, throbbing cock lodged deep inside of me, and the wild sensation the rough penetration sent through my quivering body.

I cried when he pulled halfway out, only to immediately thrust back in hard enough that I had to use all my strength to keep on my hands and knees. He didn't show me any mercy, despite the already exhausted state Lightning had left me in, and instantly set a reckless pace that had me seeing stars every time his brutal cock pounded into me.

It may have hurt, somewhere past the wild ecstasy, but all I could feel was pleasure—deep, soul changing pleasure—and a rush of power so potent it felt like fire in my blood.

It didn't matter that I didn't graduate top of my class like Trish, that I was just a blogger—it didn't matter that out in the real world, I felt insecure about who I was and what I looked like. In here, in my bed, with one of the most powerful men inside of me and another watching us, I was invincible. As many problems as we had, when we were together like this, there wasn't room for any doubt that I was as much the center of their universe as they were mine, if only for a little while.

I gritted my teeth around the high-pitched screams threatening to tear my throat raw and opened my eyes. Lightning's startling blue gaze met mine, nailing me to the spot as efficiently as The Shade did from behind. His eyes were dark with unbridled passion as he stared at me, he was fully naked, and his chest rose and fell with breaths that made his nostrils flare. For a moment I thought he was going to launch at The Shade and rip him off me to take his place, but he didn't. He simply stayed put in front of the bed, watching. From the movement of his arm I knew he was stroking his own erection, but when I dipped my gaze to look, The Shade grabbed my long hair in one hand and yanked my head back and up.

"If you're getting distracted, clearly I'm not fucking you hard enough," he grunted behind me. A resounding slap landed on my behind, but when I yelped and jolted forward his hold on my hair kept me in place. The steady tug on my roots and the sting from my ass only enhanced the raw sensation of his huge cock pounding into me, rubbing every sensitive spot exactly how I liked it.

Only when I'd completely forgotten all about looking at what Lightning might be doing did The Shade let go of my hair. His hand went straight for my clit, pressing in firmly without ever slowing his thrust.

The orgasm was near-instant.

My pussy clamped down hard on the intrusion at the pressure against my most sensitive nub, and the sensation sent me over the edge with a long cry. My vision blackened and blurred for several moments while pleasure tore through me like a near-painful inferno. I bucked and sobbed against The Shade's continued thrusts, riding out my orgasm with spasms so strong they wracked my entire body.

Thankfully, my pussy's desperate milking of his throbbing cock was enough to push him over, too.

He roared as if challenging the other male in the room with a battle cry and clutched me so tight that I could feel the rapid beat of his heart against my back for several long, wonderful moments. Then he released me, and I slid gratefully down toward the mattress with every intent on passing out, not caring that The Shade's cock was still heavy inside of my worn sheath.

"Not so fast, Kittykat." Lightning's voice was rough with urgent need when he grabbed me by the chin and pulled me back up on all four. "I need you."

I cracked open my eyes just in time to see his thick erection pointing threateningly at me.

"Get off her, Shade."

The last bit was a snarl.

The Shade growled lazily. "No. You had your go. This was the deal for you taking the first turn, and I'm not done enjoying her."

"Oh, for heaven's sake." I was too exhausted to deal with their rivalry and too sore to want to subject myself to another fucking, so I did what any sensible woman would have—I reached for Lightning's hard cock and wrapped my lips around it.

A small tremor went through the hero as my hot mouth

closed around him. "Fuck," he hissed, and tightened both hands in my tangled hair. "Fuck, babe, yes, just like that."

I had enough time to feel a small sliver of pride and power at his complete unraveling from the lightest touch of my tongue. He hissed in an odd sort of whine, and I could practically feel his struggle not to pull too hard on my hair when his hard length slid deeper into the cavern of my mouth. Then his cock pulsed against my tongue, and Lightning seemed to regain his ability to move.

He shifted his grip to my cheeks, tipping my head up a little so I could look into his eyes and his thick cock slid a little more easily down. I coughed when he neared my throat, but he didn't force me to take it all the way down.

"Would never hurt you," he gasped, as if he'd seen the worry in my eyes. "Never. Oh, *fuck*, you feel so fucking good. I'm so close, so close."

His movements became more uncontrolled, more erratic, but he kept his promise not to hurt me as he fucked my mouth with low growls and mewls of pure pleasure.

Even though I'd been ridden beyond fatigue, his obvious enjoyment made my own, otherwise thoroughly satisfied, libido start to wake. The thick cock still buried deep in my pussy didn't help matters, especially not as it was beginning to inflate again, pushing against my battered walls with increasing demand.

Maybe the unexpected spurt of desire was why I dug my nails into Lightning's hamstrings when he tried to pull away.

"I can't hold back any longer," he growled in warning when I clung to him, refusing to let him slip out of my mouth. My jaws ached from his size, but something wild and unhinged deep inside of me craved the taste of his seed, and it currently had control of my brain. Instead of pulling away like I always had when giving a guy head in the past, I tightened the seal of my lips as much as I could and sucked harder on his pulsing head.

Lightning came with a deep groan. He thrust forward, almost reaching my throat again, but managed to steady himself against the top of my head.

The first taste of his cum sent my mind spinning. It was slightly salty, I noted, and then I flew.

ELEVEN

I tore up through the roof of my apartment, ripping a jagged hole that let me look down on the bed I'd just left deep down below me. Two men were bent over a collapsed body in the middle of the tangled sheets. I laughed at how small they looked and flexed my shoulder muscles with sheer joy.

Powerful wings beat behind- and around me with the motion, and I realized they were a part of me. I had *wings!*

The night felt like a velvet caress around my scaly body. I swung around and saw the lights from the city spin underneath me, growing ever smaller and dimmer as I continued to soar higher and higher. There was nothing holding me back, nothing tying me to the ground—I was strong and powerful and *free.*

With another joyful laugh I lifted my gaze to the stars above. The night was endless. Feeling nothing but exhilaration I continued upwards. I could fly forever.

"Kathryn."

I frowned. Where did that voice come from?

"Kathryn, you need to wake up now. That's enough flying for tonight."

Wake up? What? I shook my head, irritated with the interruption. How was a girl meant to get lost between the stars like this?

Someone unseen grabbed my shoulders and shook me, and suddenly, my wings were gone.

I screamed as I dropped like a rock, flailing in the empty air for purpose, but there was nothing to grab on to. Down, down, down I fell, until the lights of the city were once again visible deep below me. Then my high rise appeared directly underneath me, with the gaping hole I'd ripped in it when I took off, and there was the bed with the three people still in it.

The girl was sprawled out spread-eagle, with a naked man on each side.

It was me.

The familiar sight of my own round face and blonde hair sent a jolt of shock through me. Then I crashed through the roof to my inescapable death.

WAKING up was like being drenched with a bucket of cold water. I sat up with a yell, panting and gasping as if I'd narrowly avoided my own death. Which I suppose falling from several miles' height and miraculously surviving would class as.

"What the heck was that?" My voice was hoarse and panting. Someone handed me a glass of water, and I grabbed it blindly and gulped down half its contents.

"That, my dear, was a high."

"A what?" I twisted my neck to look at The Shade, who was sat next to me on the bed. He was still gloriously naked, save the mask, and my frazzled brain took two full seconds to remember exactly what I'd been doing before suddenly sprouting wings. I glanced up at the ceiling. The white paint was crack-free, without the slightest hint of an impromptu skylight.

"Supe sperm. It gives mortal women a high, it would seem." Lightning reached out from behind me and planted a kiss in my hair. "Sorry about that. I did try to pull out."

I blinked. "I... You *drugged* me?"

"Yeah." He sounded way too relaxed for someone who'd just gotten his lover high.

I turned around to glare at him, only to be met by a peck on the tip of my nose.

"It sounded like you enjoyed it, though." He said, smiling mischievously. "You kept laughing manically and muttering about ant-people."

"I think you should lay back down," The Shade rumbled. "Your pupils are still blown."

I didn't resist as he maneuvered me back down between them. The room *did* seem a little off kilter.

Both men stretched out next to me, one on each side, resting on an elbow so they could look at me. They way their identical, blue eyes followed my every move made a vague note of self-consciousness set in behind the remnants of my drug haze. I bit my lip and glanced from one to the other. "Sooo... what does this mean, then? I take it I'm not too presumptuous in assuming that the fact that you two are naked and in the same bed could suggest that we need to have The Talk soon?"

There. I did it. I brought up the potential for a boyfriend-girlfriend... boyfriend talk. My nerves were surprisingly calm. Again, probably because of the lingering effects of Lightning's *super juice.* Christ.

The Shade smiled wryly and let a couple of fingers dance over my stomach, on top of the duvet. "Oh you assume so, do you?"

I huffed at him. "Well, what do I know, you two may be having threesomes together every other Saturday."

"Yeah, no, not exactly," Lightning grunted from my other side. "We'll talk, Kathryn, I promise. But not now. You're still high, and we need to figure out... some stuff before we talk to you."

There was always something, wasn't there? With a defeated sigh I closed my eyes and let the exhaustion crawl in over my body like a heavy blanket. Maybe once the mayor and Bright had been defeated we would actually be able to sit down and work out what exactly was going on between us, but until then, I'd be best off pretending like my heart wasn't glowing with happiness from the way both men wrapped their arms around me as my mind started to drift. Saying out loud how badly in love with the two mortal enemies I was would only make everything all the more complicated.

THE SKY ABOVE ST. Anthony had just started to brighten ever so slightly when I woke up again, this time to a dull but pleasant ache between my legs and joints so stiff I thought I might need to have them oiled in order to ever move normally again.

I twisted my neck to glance out through the window

nearest my bed, and had my line of sight obstructed by a large, male figure. I frowned and squinted at my bed companion in the still-darkened room. It was The Shade, and he was fast asleep, with one bulging arm resting casually around my waist.

I would have never thought he would let his guard down enough to actually fall asleep around me. Or his enemy, for that matter. I looked to my other side, and saw Lightning laying sprawled out next to me, with his hand on my thigh underneath the duvet. He was also completely gone.

So, what, one night of debauched sex with the same woman and they now trusted each other enough to pass out cold in the same bed?

I stared at the sleeping hero's masked face, and felt a strong urge to sneak a peak. I already knew that the masked man on my other side pretended to be a rich tycoon by day, but Lightning... I had no idea who he was. And if I would even recognize him.

I leaned in a little closer and let my fingers hover over his mask. He would never have to know that I'd looked.

But *I* would know. And I would know that, when Lightning had allowed himself to be vulnerable around me, I had broken his trust.

With a deep sigh I removed my hand and sat up. I couldn't do that to him. Even if all his *"my woman!"* hollering turned out to be rooted in nothing more than the odd sexual attraction between us. Yeah, that talk really couldn't happen soon enough.

An urgent reminder that I hadn't visited the bathroom after our escapades last night made my thoughts turn to more immediate concerns. Carefully, so to not wake the sleeping men, I extracted myself from the bed, wincing for every painful movement. The Shade growled disapprovingly when I slipped out from underneath his arm, but didn't wake up fully. He was breathing deeply and evenly again before I was more than two steps from the bed.

Even superhumans fell victim to sex comas, it would seem.

I made my way to the bathroom on wobbly legs, and my muscles' weakness didn't feel like it was entirely down to the thorough fucking I'd received. Perhaps there was still a small bit of whatever high I'd been on after swallowing Lightning's semen left in my system. Narcotic sperm. Jesus-effing-Christ, there should be a manual for humans embarking on any sort of relationship with a supe. I'd been so convinced I was on a wild flight toward the stars, and all because I'd felt like tasting the *goods*.

The sky was growing lighter when I came out from the bathroom, teeth cleaned and certain areas washed free of sticky reminders of my wild night, but the sun had yet to rise. I had every intention of slipping back into bed between the two gloriously naked men still passed out on it, and maybe see if I could catch a few more hours of sleep before we had to get up and deal with the whole mayor-Bright problem, but just as I passed my desk, my phone lit up.

A new text.

I frowned at the display as it went dark again. Who in the heck would think to text me this early in the morning? It wasn't like my phone usually blew up with incoming texts and calls, and certainly never at this time of day.

It was too odd to wait until later, even though I wanted nothing more than to crawl back into bed, so I snatched my phone up and checked the message.

It was from Trish, and simply said: "*Are you alone?*"

I frowned and typed back: "No, *but they're sleeping. What's up?*"

A few moments later, her response ticked in: "*Remember the reporter I said was interested in the case? He wants to meet you, now. Without your boyfriends knowing. Can you get away?*"

I glanced at the bed. They'd both be absolutely furious if I just took off, but getting a big-time reporter Trish obviously trusted from the biggest network in town would be a massive boon. And as much as I appreciated the supes' protection, I hadn't signed up to be the designated damsel in distress, whose only contribution was to faint in the corner while the men worked everything out. I needed to meet this guy, and if he was leery of superhumans, well... I couldn't blame him. And I also couldn't drag The Shade and Lightning along.

"*Okay. I'll leave his name on a note for them, though, or they're gonna tear the city apart if they wake up before I'm back. Who is he?*"

The pause before Trish texted back this time was considerably longer.

"*It's Nick Coleman. Meet us down by the harbor, by Macnillan's old steel factory. And Kat, you can't tell your 'friends' where you're going, or Coleman will bail. He doesn't want anyone there but you and me.*"

I gaped at my screen for a full minute. Nick Coleman? Nick-freaking-*Coleman?* As far as reporters went, he was as much of a rock star as they came. Everyone who ever took a single journalism class in college wanted to be him. He was the embodiment of justice, was famous for always getting the story, and had even won a Pulitzer for his work. If St. Anthony had a non-superhuman hero, it was Nick Coleman.

A sliver of relief found its way in past the awe. Maybe it

was a bit ridiculous to have more faith in a human reporter than two supes, but somehow having Nick Coleman on my side made me feel like everything was going to be fine—it was a bit like if the president called up to say he was going to personally deal with harassment in your office. Shit was going to get *done*.

I got dressed as quickly and quietly as I could, because I made myself no delusions that if either supe woke up, I would be going anywhere—and then pulled out a piece of paper and a pen from my desk.

Shade, Lightning,
   Trish called. She got Nick Coleman to help us. I'm off meeting him now. I'll be back before midday.
   Kathryn

THERE. While they would undoubtedly still get pissed that I'd taken off, at least they knew who I was with and when I'd be back. I was being responsible, without also being completely useless.

When I snuck out of the apartment and closed the door quietly behind me, they were both still sleeping peacefully. With a little luck, I'd even make it back before they ever woke up.

IT WAS FULLY daylight when I made it to the harbor, but the sun was hiding behind a thick layer of gray clouds, setting a gloomy ambiance.

Macnillan's closed-down steel factory was located at the edge of the industrial quarter, and I couldn't suppress a shudder as I skirted the empty, looming warehouses. I would never be able to see the run-down buildings here again, without remembering what it felt like to be running for my life and knowing there was no out.

"Kat!"

I looked up at the shout, and smiled when I saw Trish step out from behind the steel factory. Her black hair danced in the wind, and she looked tense as she huddled in her coat against the cool winds blowing off the river behind her.

"A nice, warm cafe would have been a lot more pleasant," I joked as I walked up to her and pushed my hands into my pockets. "Just sayin'."

She returned my smile, but it didn't reach her eyes. "Yeah, sure. Nick didn't want to be seen with us, though. He's afraid Bright might figure out he's involved, then."

I frowned. Surely he was going to anchor the story, so why would he not want to risk Bright finding out? I was about to ask, but then shrugged it off. Maybe he just wanted to wait until we had some definitive proof. He didn't have two superhuman protectors, after all.

"Is he on his way?" I asked, squinting up at the gray sky. "The sooner I'm back, the less chance I'll get grounded like a kid. I'm telling ya, as thankful as I am for Lightning and The Shade's protection, they aren't half overbearing."

"He is indeed," a deep voice sounded behind me.

I jumped and shrieked, then giggled at my overzealous reaction. "Sorry, you startled me!"

I turned around to face Nick, smile still plastered across my face, but where I'd expected to see the famous reporter's trademark wide jaw and golden head of hair, a feathery mask met me instead.

My smile faded as I knitted my brows in confusion. Mirome stood in front of me, as flamboyantly dressed as ever, with an arrogant smirk on his thin lips.

"Are you... Nick Coleman?" Even as I said the words, they made little sense. If he was, then why was he revealing his disguise to me? And to Trish?

Mirome laughed—a cold, mocking laugh. "As if *I* would have the time or inclination to infiltrate your human society like that. Why don't you explain the situation to your little *friend,* Patricia?"

I frowned deeper and turned back to Trish. Whatever was going on, I had the distinct impression that I'd somehow missed something vital. "What's going on? I don't understand?"

Trish no longer looked nervous. She looked at me with calm and... distaste? The shock that went through me when I recognized the look of loathing in her gaze jolted me out of the confusion. Cold, instinctive fear gripped me instead.

"You never did have any clue. Not back in college, and not now. Poor, slow Kat never understood much of anything," she spat. "You picked the wrong side. Maybe if you would have grasped how powerful Bright is, you would have supported him rather than try to help those two glorified action figures you let into your bed."

It was obvious what she was saying, but even through the chilling clarity of her confession, my heart refused to believe it. There had to be some other explanation, some rational reason for what she was saying—

"He picked me, you know. *Me.*" The disgust in her expression turned to pride. "I suppose I should thank you. He discovered me when I was looking into your claims about the mayor. If it hadn't been for your little story, maybe he would never have found me."

The confusion dispersed with a near-audible snap, making way for crispy-clear and chilling understanding.

"Bright claimed you." It wasn't a question. I stared at my best friend and finally *saw* her. She wasn't the same girl I'd stayed up late nights revising with back in our college years. She hadn't been the same girl for years, but now... now there was darkness in her eyes. I remembered Mirome's human, the one who had been so very proud of his servitude, and knew I had lost her.

"I am to be his bride," Trish said. She seemed lost in her fervent dreams of the future Bright had undoubtedly manipulated her into believing in. "I will be by his side while he rules this city. There will be no other woman with as much power as I."

I wanted to cry. To scream. To somehow fight the superhuman who was pacing beside us, that arrogant little smirk plastered across his face as if he knew how delusional she was being while only letting her sink deeper and deeper under her superhuman master's spell. But I didn't have time. I needed to figure a way out of this mess, and I needed to do it now, while Trish was too busy ranting about her powerful new master to stop me.

Only I knew I couldn't escape. Mirome would be able to catch me within two steps if I tried to run, and I wasn't strong enough to fight off a superhuman.

If only I had a way of contacting Lightning or—

My heart skipped a beat when I remembered that I *did* have a way of contacting them.

At the mayor's ball, when Elias Shaw had asked for my phone number, he had given me his in return. And I'd typed it into my contact list. Only... even if, by some miracle, the Shade kept the same phone on him when he was masked as he used when he was in his human disguise, then... then he would realize that I knew who he was.

As much as I saw something good in him that no one else in the city did, I wasn't entirely sure that he would let me live with that knowledge. He might like me, but allow a loose end that could end him by spilling his secret to the wrong person to walk around freely? That didn't sound like something the infamous criminal would ever do, no matter how fond he may be of my body.

I glanced at Mirome, who was watching Trish rant on about Bright with a bored expression.

But my only other option was guaranteed death. At least Lightning might be able to save me from The Shade's wrath, whereas if I took my chances with Mirome... and Bright... There was only one outcome.

As quietly as I could, I reached into my pocket and fumbled for my phone. I kept glancing at Mirome to see if he was watching me while I desperately tried to unlock my phone without making too much movement. A wave of relief shot through me when I finally got to push the right button. Now, just to navigate to my contact list...

It was the one time in my life being a bit of a loner paid off. I didn't have too many contacts to memorize as I scrolled all the way down to "S," and I was 99% sure I got the right name without looking when I pressed "Call." What I was less sure of was whether or not The Shade would answer.

"I'm sorry it has to be this way." Trish's change in tone brought my attention back to her.

I pulled my hand from my pocket and looked at her pleadingly. Perhaps it wasn't too late—perhaps I could reach her somehow, if only I tried. "It doesn't have to be this way, Trish. You're my friend—my only real friend. Don't do this. Bright, he's only using you. He's messing with your mind. They can do that, with their pheromon—"

The stinging slap came out of nowhere. Pain burst through my cheek, and the impact made my jaw snap shut, effectively silencing me.

"*Shut. Up!*" Trish glared at me, hand still raised. Her eyes were black with sudden rage, and her pretty face was all twisted in anger. "You don't get to speak about him like that! He loves me, and I love him. Not all of us are too thick to form real relationships. Don't put your shortcomings on me! Just because no one will ever really love *you* doesn't mean you get to disparage *my* relationship. He and I are one —and you are *nothing,* like you always were! Do you know why I'm the only one who still keeps in touch with you? It's because I *pity* you! No one else could be bothered, because you're so pathetic, Kat. You always were and you always will be. And it's your own damn fault you're going to die. If you hadn't dropped your panties at the first supe who showed you any sort of interest, Bright wouldn't care one whiff about you."

Tears blurred my vision of my only friend as she glared at me with murderous rage, hands fisted into balls as she panted.

Everything she'd said, I had feared at one point or another, but always managed to push away. I was awkward, and a loner by nature, and she was the only friend from college who had stayed in any sort of contact. I had always wondered if this was the reason.

My cheek hurt, but so did my heart. My best friend... It wasn't just Bright's influence. It couldn't be. This much hatred couldn't just come from his claim.

Then, unexpectedly, anger welled up, drowning out the hurt. If that was how she'd felt about me all along, then I wasn't the one who was pathetic. She had lied to me for so many years, faked her friendship—and now, she was willing to *kill* me, simply because a man told her to?

"*You* are the pathetic one!" I hissed, balling my own hands into fists as I glared back through my tears. "And you're a fake, a liar and now an accomplice to murder. Well done, Trish. I hope you'll remember this moment when you realize that you are nothing more than a toy to him. And you!" I turned halfway around so I could stare Mirome down. In my surging anger, I didn't care that he was a super-human who could end me with a flick of his wrist. If I was going to die, I was going down swinging.

"They trusted you! You were their teacher. Their friend! That's the only thing they agree on. How can you betray them like this?"

Mirome took my angry assault with complete and utter calm. He clucked his tongue and shook his head at me as I glared up at him, wishing I was strong enough to wring his neck for the betrayal against the two men who had claimed my heart.

"I am not *betraying* my old students, little dimwit. I am merely ensuring that I don't get on Bright's wrong side. And if they'd had any sense, they would have heeded my warning and done the same. It's either be on his side, or perish, and I have no intention of ending my existence for the sake of opposing a man who simply wants what is our race's birthright. You humans—you are so inferior in your imperfections that you will never grasp it. Why should we live in the shadows? Cower at the thought of angering lesser beings than ourselves?

"I am not too surprised that Lightning is trying to be noble and '*save humankind*'. Saddened, but not surprised. But that The Shade has chosen to follow him in his ridiculous hero complex? That is an unexpected loss—and one I will hold you fully responsible for, you worthless cunt."

The abrupt change from his calm, overbearing tone to the utter malice in his final statement shocked me, and when what was visible of his face twisted into a mask of hatred, my own anger fizzled and died, overtaken by instinctive fear. In his blue eyes, I saw nothing but murderous intent.

"W-what do you mean?" I breathed as cold dread took over my body, freezing me in place.

Mirome scoffed. "As if you didn't already know. You are their mate—their '*soulmate*,' as you humans so poetically call it, and neither would ever allow you to be unhappy. Your ridiculous attempt to expose Bright has brought them down with you, and they don't even care that they are slaves to a simple, human cunt. And that, my dear, is why I am going to personally kill you, once Bright has used you to lure them into his trap."

He was mad. Stark, raving mad. I saw it in his hateful eyes as he lifted his hand and brought it down, and felt it in my very bones as his fist impacted with the side of my head.

Blackness exploded out from my temple, wrapped in red-hot pain.

And then there was nothing.

Read the thrilling conclusion of the Darkness series in

Fires in the Darkness

I am out of time.

There is no more waiting, no more hiding in the shadows. No more pretending I don't love the two men who have claimed me as theirs.

But darkness has arrived.

And if we don't fight it... If it wins....

I will lose my soul.

CONNECT WITH NORA

Want to chat all things alpha? (and ruthlessly sexy book-boyfriends in general?)

Join Nora's Reader's Group:

EMAIL:
www.nora-ash.com/newsletter

ALSO BY NORA ASH

THE OMEGA PROPHECY

Ragnarök Rising

Weaving Fate

Betraying Destiny

DEMON'S MARK

Branded

Demon's Mark

Prince of Demons

ALPHA TIES

Alpha

Feral

ANCIENT BLOOD

Origin

Wicked Soul

Debt of Bones*

DARKNESS

Into the Darkness

Hidden in Darkness

Shades of Darkness

Fires in the Darkness

MADE & BROKEN

Dangerous

Monster

Trouble